ONCE CHARMED, TWICE CURSED

SHAYLIN GANDHI

Also by Shaylin Gandhi

Contemporary Romance

When We Had Forever

Fantasy Romance

The Assassin's Song

Song of the Hundred-Year Summer

For More

For free books, bonus content, ARC opportunities, and subscriber-only updates, join my newsletter:

shaylingandhi.com/news

Chapter One

There's only one man I want to marry, and he isn't one of the ninety-nine who have proposed.

I stand by the window in our grandiose second-floor hallway, staring out at the graveled drive below. Today is the last day any prospective husbands can make an offer for me.

Tomorrow, my brother will decide who I'll marry.

At the thought, my breathing accelerates. The drive outside is empty, as is the road beyond, and the sun is already making a rapid dive toward the trees. But before the day ends, there *will* be a hundredth proposal. Any moment now, Weston Wildes will come stomping up the road, his golden brows pulled low over the eyes that never fail to drive a shiver through me.

I can see it already. Weston will let himself into our home without so much as a knock, the same way he always does. He'll clomp upstairs and glower at my brother because he glowers at everyone, then clap Brendan on the back to let him know they're still friends, regardless. The ease with which they touch one another will make my chest ache. The ease with which Weston touches everyone but me.

But then will come the moment. My favorite moment. Weston will peer past Brendan, searching. His gaze will collide with mine.

I'll forget how to breathe. The knowledge will desert me just as readily the thousandth time as the first, and I'll stand transfixed, my entire body kindling under that piercing stare.

Brendan will start yammering about finances, but Weston will hold up a hand, halting my brother mid-sentence. He'll step past and come close to me. Closer than propriety strictly allows, but not so close that we risk touching. He'll rummage in the pocket of his modest tailcoat and produce a careworn book, one he probably spent half an hour choosing for me.

At the sight of it, my heart will threaten to overflow. My brother will try to ruin the moment by mocking his best friend for indulging my love of stories, but only because Brendan never catches the way Weston's glower eases when we're close like this. He won't see how the ruthless angles of that beautiful face soften only for me.

Weston will hand me the book. He'll ensure our fingers don't brush, even though he will have pulled on his gloves, like he always does when he's in this house.

I'll smile. Pretend not to imagine what his hand would feel like against mine, the warmth of it.

"Hello, Birdie," Weston will say. He'll do it in that way of his, like my nickname is a secret he's keeping from the rest of the world. Then we'll talk, and he won't once let his gaze stray downward. He'll ignore my Mark entirely, and I'll marvel at the effort, because every gown I own boasts a neckline low enough to put the triquetra between my collarbones on prominent display.

But Weston will study my face. Only my face.

Once he's told me why I'll love the story he's brought—and he'll be right, he's always right—Weston will follow my brother upstairs to his office. On the third floor, they'll talk accounting and business and boxing, and then the man I've loved for a decade, the one I fell for on sight at fourteen, will finally muster the courage to ask for me.

Weston will be the last man to propose. The hundredth. And the only one who actually matters.

"Bria."

I turn at the sound of my name. My brother stands amid the hallway's opulence, his hands loose at his sides. His satin waistcoat gleams in the slanted light. "Is there a reason you're standing there, staring out the window?"

I shift my weight. "I'm waiting."

An easy smile tilts his mouth. "For?"

The answer swirls in my veins, filling the spaces between my ribs. *Weston*, I want to say. *Freedom.*

But Brendan has no idea I've spent the last decade yearning for the one man I'm not allowed to touch. For the gift only Weston can give me.

I'm not sure what he would do if he did.

"To see if anyone else comes," I hedge.

My brother chuckles and wanders over. The late light deepens the green of his eyes and gilds the streaks in his light brown hair. I imagine it does the same to me, because our coloring is identical, enough that when we were younger, people often mistook us for twins. In actuality, Brendan is a year older, but as children, we stuck so closely to one another that people assumed we shared a birthday.

That was *before*, though. Before I retreated into books, and my brother into things like satin waistcoats and matched cutlery sets.

Brendan studies the window, using its reflection to arrange his hair into a more stylish configuration. "There's no one left, Bria. Every man in Pine's End has already thrown his hat into the ring."

I inspect the drive. It's still empty, but with any luck, Weston will round the bend in the road in moments.

And that's the thing—when it comes to luck, I have lots. I have all the luck in the world, in fact.

The fortune goddess decided so herself, before I was even born. She inked her three-pointed knot onto my skin when I was still in the womb, marking me as one of her favored.

Good luck has followed me ever since. When I was three, a freak storm leveled half of Pine's End, but my family remained unaffected, our home the only one without so much as a shingle blown out of place.

When I was seven, I went digging for crabs at the seashore and unearthed a chest of gold instead, stashed there by some long-ago pirate. The found fortune allowed us to move from the humble industrial town of Pine's End to this lavish country estate six miles southward, where my parents now count dukes and lords among their neighbors.

And my luck hasn't ended there. It spills over onto those around me. Whenever I pass by in the street, people find lost trinkets in their pockets, or remember things they'd tried desperately not to forget. In the market, a vendor might knock a carton of eggs from a table, only for it to land unharmed in my basket. Someone will cast a handful of dice in my presence and come up with exactly the roll they wanted.

Serendipity billows off me like perfume, and anyone standing close enough can inhale a bit for themselves.

Hence the ninety-nine offers of marriage.

It's not because those men actually care about me. None of them even know me. Not really.

"Not *every* man," I tell Brendan.

My brother's smile turns puzzled. "There are a hundred bachelors in Pine's End. You've had ninety-nine proposals. Surely you can do the math."

I lift my eyebrows and give him a significant look.

His smile dims. "You can't mean... Come on. Not *Weston*."

My fingers tremble, and I bury them in my skirts to hide the tell. I've never dared to confront Brendan about my feelings for his best friend. Truth be told, I've never really dared to confront anyone about anything. My luck has always tilted the world in such a way that I haven't had to. Everything always comes to me.

Everything except Weston, that is.

"Well, why not?" I say.

Brendan's gaze narrows. "Bria. That isn't funny."

"Who said I was joking?"

"I did," he says crisply. "Forget that he's my best friend and I'd break his nose if he so much as sniffed at you in that way. He's a *Null*, Bria. I know you two are friendly, but you can never forget his Mark."

I press my lips together. I haven't forgotten Weston's curse. Or the terrible luck that plagues him because of it. I never do. "I know. I only thought that... That maybe..." A fist closes around my windpipe, and my courage dries up. Damnit.

Brendan cocks his head. "What? You figured he'd like having you around to cancel his curse all the time? That you might avoid a real marriage by working out some sort of friendship situation with him?"

Shock nearly pinches my throat shut. "What? No, I—"

"First off, he has no money to offer," Brendan says, as if I haven't even spoken. "He may be the most brilliant accountant in Pine's End, but he can't compete with what the others have promised, not on his salary. Even if he could, no man is going to marry a woman he can never touch."

I do my best not to flinch, but Brendan may as well have just slapped me across the face.

My brother's eyes drop to my neckline. I squash the urge to plaster my hands over my triquetra, because there's no point in trying to hide my Mark. Or the dismayed heat creeping up my chest.

He sighs. "Look, I know you want to help him, but his Mark is his problem, not yours. Even if he could offer for you, even if he swore to give you your own room and be your husband only in name, I'd never put you in that position. All he'd have to do is touch your hand for a minute. He'd be so tempted. Sooner or later, he'd slip. And you're too valuable for that."

My throat burns. "My Mark is too valuable, you mean?"

"Right. Yes."

Hurt yanks at my insides. Suddenly, I want to push him. Knock him down and shout that my worth as a human and as a vehicle of divine favor are *not* one and the same.

That I amount to more than this tattoo at my collar.

But emotion clogs my throat, walling off the words, so I turn back to the window. Weston will come. He has to. I've never wished this hard for something and not gotten it.

Another half-minute slinks by, but the drive remains vacant. So does the road, and when the sun kisses the tree-tops, bitter doubts creep in.

The fortune goddess can't actually help me with this, I realize. No amount of divine luck in the world can affect Weston Wildes.

Because he's Marked, too. Except his triquetra—an inverted version of mine—marks him as a Null. Not blessed by Fortuna, but forsaken. Bad luck follows him as faithfully as favor follows me, though when we stand close enough, our magic temporarily cancels out.

If we ever touched each other... We'd both lose our luck, good and bad. Forever.

My yearning for him swells into something monstrous. Maybe I can't wish Weston here through magic, but he'll come for me, even without Fortuna's intervention. Ten years of heated looks and loaned books and sheer, unadulterated longing can't possibly end with me marrying someone else. Can they?

Brendan checks his pocket watch and sighs. "Look, I know you weren't thrilled about Mom and Dad deciding you should marry, but you might as well let this idea about Weston go. He's fighting tonight, anyway."

I jolt. "He's *what?*"

"Fighting. In town. At the cotton mill."

I almost choke. "What? Are you sure?"

"Positive."

"But...he didn't tell me that."

My brother frowns. "Why would he?"

"Because," I say, unable to scrub the alarm from my voice. "I should be there. I have to be there."

Without me nearby, Weston's Mark will be in full effect. And for all his surly grace, for all that he can absorb a punch without flinching, something will happen to throw the match. A section of the ceiling will collapse as he prepares to land the winning blow, or someone will spark a cigarette and accidentally burn the place down. A floorboard will give way under Weston's feet, and he'll fall and break his neck. Something.

"I have to go," I say.

Brendan shakes his head. "What? No, you don't."

"I do. He'll lose without me there."

"So he'll lose." His eyes narrow. "Honestly, what's gotten into you? He fights all the time without you there. This is no different."

That brings me up short. Weston always invites me to his matches. Or so I thought. "He fights without me? *Regularly?*"

"Why do you sound so surprised?"

Bitterness floods my tongue. "Has he ever won? When he was on his own?"

Brendan rubs a hand across his jaw. "Once, maybe. Twice? But that's not the point. The point is that he's a grown man. He can make his own decisions. Without you."

A burn takes up residence in my chest and spreads outward. I have to get to Weston. Keep him safe. I don't care what Brendan says.

I turn on my heel and sail down the hall. I've already wasted half the afternoon standing at this window like an idiot, and Weston is probably getting his face punched in as we speak.

"Bria! Where are you going?"

"To help Weston win," I call back.

"Stop."

I don't. I don't even slow. I just hurry down the staircase and out into the cooling evening, then make for the stables. No time to bother with a cloak.

I saddle my yellow mare and vault into the stirrups, then bolt out into the falling darkness.

As the manor retreats and Pine's End draws nearer, betrayal slices across my heart. Weston isn't coming for me. He never was, and I don't know what that means. How that could possibly be. How he could let Brendan marry me off to someone who doesn't even care about me.

Nor do I know what I'll do once I reach him, because I've never had to fight for anything before. I'm not sure I even know where to start.

But I am certain of one thing.

I'll do everything—*everything*—in my power to keep Weston's luck from hurting him.

Chapter Two

When I arrive, the cotton mill is packed.

The machinery has been shut down for the day and hauled to the floor's edges, clearing a ring in the center of the room, though I can't get a proper look with so many people here. Dozens of men jostle against one another, their foreheads glinting, their shirtsleeves rolled to their elbows. Here and there, jewel-toned skirts flash in the crowd, but for the most part, the place reeks of excitement and male bodies.

I wade into the chaos. Or try to, but those who notice me inevitably edge closer instead of further away. Eyes drop to my Mark as if pulled there.

Heat stains my cheeks. These men are probably only looking at my triquetra, but I never really know, considering its proximity to my neckline.

"Excuse me, please," I say, but laughter and shouted bets swallow up my words.

A nearby man takes pity on me. He cups his mouth with work-roughened hands. "Move! Let the lady through!"

At that, the crowd parts—barely—and I squeeze forward.

Someone trails calloused fingers along my forearms. Another someone grazes my neck with the back of a hand.

The touches are innocent, I know. Just a few bold souls trying to glean some luck, and none of them would actually grope me. They wouldn't dare. Not after Weston broke four of Theodore Cavanaugh's fingers last year—not to mention two of his ribs *and* his nose—after Theodore told half of Pine's End he'd taken my virginity.

I'd never seen Weston as furious as when he made Theodore take it all back. In public.

Even though it wasn't actually a lie.

The sea of bodies closes in again. The temperature ratchets upward until my blood simmers. Am I too late? Judging by the wet-sounding cracks echoing off the rafters, the fight is already underway.

Ragged cheers erupt. My less-than-impressive stature prevents me from seeing much, but luckily, the crowd shifts, granting me a sightline. And there he is. Weston Wildes.

My heart goes into freefall.

The moment imprints itself on my mind. He's bare from the waist up, save for the linen strips wrapped around his hands. I've caught him mid-punch, one fist stretched while the other guards his chin, and it's...breathtaking. He's all long, clean lines and tanned skin, golden hair and angry eyes. His triquetra glints between his collarbones. The inverted point leads my eyes downward, over his sculpted chest and serrated abdomen, then to the twin lines that slant into his breeches.

Fortuna's blessings, Theodore didn't even begin to compare.

Which probably explains why I chose him. Because he

didn't matter. Because no one will ever matter like this man does.

Weston's fist connects, and the world leaps into motion again. The other fighter's head snaps back. Crimson droplets spray, but whoever the man is, he keeps his feet.

Impressive.

Weston tucks his fists and retreats a few feet, circling with the focus of a tiger preparing to pounce. If not for his Mark, he'd probably win most every fight, because he's lethal. Poised. He's fury cloaked in strength.

In other words, entirely different in the ring than he is with me.

The crowd in front of me shifts, blocking my view again. Something happens that makes everyone shout at once.

Panic flickers along my nerves. Weston looked fine a second ago, but that Mark of his invites misfortune. He courts disaster just by existing.

Someone lands a punch. The cheering intensifies. I push and shove, but I might as well hurl myself against a stone wall for all that the crowd yields.

Damnit. Ten more feet, and the radius of my magic would touch Weston's. Our opposing forces would momentarily cancel out, but I can't get close enough.

I wedge myself between two bodies and glimpse Weston knocking his opponent to the floor. He raises a fist. Muscle and sinew strain.

The din reaches a fever pitch, and for a second, I dare to hope he'll win. That his abundance of skill will trump the odds forever stacked against him.

But something flashes overhead, yanking my gaze up to the rafters. There's a...*housecat* up there, stalking along the beam over the ring. The animal looks innocent enough, but I know better.

When it comes to Weston Wildes, nothing is innocent. Or random.

My gaze skims along the rafter, then slams to a stop. A pit opens in my stomach. A hatchet lies in the cat's path, directly atop the beam. Someone left a freaking *axe* up there, probably while making repairs. Now all it will take is one jostle of feline paws to send the hatchet plummeting onto some hapless victim below.

I know exactly who it will be, of course.

A gnarled cry rips from my throat. "Move! Let me through!"

But the fight has reached its pinnacle, and every eye is glued to the arena. I search frantically for something to throw. I'll knock that cat to its death before I'll see a blade buried in Weston's skull.

But there's nothing at hand. Just men, frenzied shouts, and the stench of perspiration.

Desperation turns my insides to water. With no other options, I drop to my hands and knees and crawl through the sea of breech-clad legs. I have to get to Weston. Insulate him with my luck. And I have to do it *now*.

Surprised shouts accompany my frantic burrowing. My lace skirts snag against the floorboards as splinters lance into my knees, but I don't care. I'd rather shred this dress to ribbons than let that hatchet fall. From that height, it could kill him. Easily.

Fear throttles my airway as I squeeze between two pairs of polished black boots. No one steps on me, though. Not that they would. I'm too lucky for that.

The forest of legs thins. Suddenly, I'm free, my heart screaming as I stumble to my feet just inside the ring.

Weston freezes.

"Birdie?" he says, like he can't believe I'm standing in front him.

My gaze flies to the ceiling, but it's too late. The cat knocks the hatchet loose, sending the thing hurtling.

It arcs through empty space.

It's headed straight for Weston.

Chapter Three

I throw myself at Weston, fueled by an instinct that directs my muscles without needing input from my brain.

The hatchet spins, a lethal whirl of steel, and I shout a silent prayer. I'm close enough now to cancel Weston's luck, but that means he's canceled mine, too.

Whatever happens next comes down to chance.

In another situation, that might feel thrilling. Freeing. But right now, someone's stripped me of my armor and pressed a dagger to my breast.

Maybe they'll stab me, maybe they won't.

Our bodies collide. Weston staggers. We go tumbling, my skirts a flurry of taffeta and lace. I land squarely on top of him, our faces inches apart.

His eyes widen as he gazes up at me. I brace, awaiting the bite of a blade in my back, but a dull thunk sounds somewhere behind me. When I turn, the hatchet glints, its head buried so deeply in the floor that a fresh split runs down the plank.

My pulse squeezes. Weston was standing there a moment ago. *Right* there.

"Birdie," he whispers. "What're you doing?"

I turn back, but he's no longer looking at my face. His gaze jumps from my arms to my collarbones, then to the swell of my bosom. He catalogs every inch of exposed skin, a frantic light shining in his eyes.

But my dress has cushioned my fall, my splayed skirts sandwiched between us. My palms sting against the rough floorboards, but no part of me touches any part of him. Not directly, at least. And directly is what matters.

When he realizes it, his gaze flicks up to mine again. For the second time in as many moments, my mind empties of thought.

Fortuna's blessings, I've never been this close to him before. Never realized he has gold flecks nestled amid the amber of his irises.

For a breathless moment, we just stare at one another. The crowd has fallen silent. All eyes take our measure, frozen as we are in our precarious position on the floor.

Then Weston gives a sharp shake of his head, as if clearing his thoughts. "Off. You have to get off."

"I'm fine," I say.

"You're not." Panic laces his voice. "I could touch you. I could *hurt* you."

When I don't move, he levers himself upward, careful not to brush against me. His broad shoulders flex with the effort of supporting both our weights.

Before he can fully rise, his opponent strides over and grips my elbow, hauling me to my feet. Weston shoots the man a look that's half glower, half gratitude.

Something about that tears me down the middle. For so long, I've told myself he would come for me. I've held out hope that someday, we would profess our feelings, and when we did, we'd put this decade of enforced distance behind us. We'd throw the rules out the window. Set each other free. Live as a man and wife are meant to.

Weston could have achieved that so easily just now. He could have laid an unseen finger against my wrist. Held on until our triquetras faded, never to return.

But he looks petrified by the near miss. So terrified of unraveling my luck that he'd rather see some other man's hands on me than his own.

I gulp down the knot of emotion blocking my throat. Stupid. This is stupid. I almost lost him just now, and here I am, wallowing in self-pity.

Weston brushes himself off, then scans me. His expression darkens. "You're hurt."

I glance down. A shard of wood has pierced my forearm and now leaks a trickle of blood. But it barely hurts. Not compared to the disappointment currently taking a bite out of my heart.

"It's nothing," I say.

He scowls. "It's not nothing."

I shoot a pointed look at the hatchet buried not two feet from where he's standing. "It could have been worse."

"Yes." His brows lower as his temper rises. "It could have. You could've been killed. And for what, Birdie? What're you even doing here?"

I reel back, stung. For what? For *what?* Is he serious?

The man who picked me up off the floor leans close.

"There's antiseptic in my office," he says softly. "You're welcome to use it, Miss Bria."

I blink at him. He looks vaguely familiar—black hair, blue eyes, sturdy features that fall just short of handsome. His name is Calder, I think, and he's the mill's foreman. I also think he offered Brendan half a year's pay for the privilege of marrying me.

I cut my gaze away, not wanting to look at him. I don't want to look at any of them. Not right now.

"Come on." Weston's tone is gruff. Something in his expression shutters. "Let's clean you up."

He spins on his heel and starts toward the back of the mill, clearly expecting me to follow.

Which I do, more out of frustration than any sense of obedience. The crowd parts to avoid Weston, even though with me close on his heels, his bad luck won't overflow onto anyone else.

For a moment, I wonder what that feels like. To have the entire world recoil as you pass.

Does Weston even notice, anymore?

He leads me to a dingy back office. He shuts the door, muting the murmurs from outside.

"What the hell were you thinking?" he growls, rounding on me. "You could've died."

My pulse kicks, anger singing in the spaces between heartbeats. "Me? *Me?* What about you? That thing would've fallen on you, if not for me. Why on earth didn't you tell me you were fighting tonight? Why would you even agree to this without making sure I'd be here to nullify your Mark?"

"Why?" Golden eyes flash. "*Why?* Is that a real question?"

"Of course it is," I spit.

He crosses his arms over his glorious chest. "Come on, Birdie, why do you think?"

"I don't know!" My words carry a bite, and I press my tongue against the roof of my mouth to stem my rising fury. He could have been hurt. He could have been *killed*. Nulls rarely live as long as Weston already has, and knowing he tempted fate tonight makes me want to hit him.

He makes an irate sound, but something deeper than anger shimmers in his eyes. "You *should* know. Because you're not a thing. You're not some tool for me to just...use at my convenience. You're a person. With your own life. And you were supposed to be busy tonight."

That shuts me up. It's everything I dream of hearing, but right now, the words only bloom cold in my bloodstream.

He was avoiding me today. On purpose.

"Busy," I say icily. "What would I be busy with?"

"Making plans. With Brendan." He slants his gaze away. "Choosing who to say yes to."

For a moment, I can't breathe. I wanted so badly to believe he'd forgotten. That he would've remembered tomorrow and come. "You knew," I say, unable to wipe the hurt from my voice. "You knew what today was, and you chose to come *here*."

His brows pull together. "Of course I did. Where else would I have gone?"

My chin trembles and my eyes sting, but I push the reaction down. All these years, I've imagined I glimpsed the same longing in him that I harbor in my own heart. Time and again, he's brought me books. He's shattered men's bones for the sake of my reputation. Those amber eyes have tracked me across the room a thousand times without cutting away.

That can't have meant nothing, can it?

When I don't answer, his scowl deepens. "Where else would I have gone, Bria?"

A hurt sound sneaks from my throat. He never calls me Bria. With him, I'm Birdie, always Birdie, ever since that time I was fifteen and he was sixteen and we came across a hatchling fallen from its nest. I brought the bird home and spent weeks nourishing it on a diet of milk-soaked bread. On the day I set it free, Weston declared me such a capable nursemaid that I must be part bird myself.

"Don't call me that," I say.

"Where else would I have gone?" he repeats, his tone dark.

"You could've come," I snap. The quiver in my voice betrays me, but I can't hold back. I'm too angry. Too wounded. Too...everything. "You could've *asked*. You're the only man who didn't."

He freezes. "Asked? Asked what?"

I mash my lips together.

He starts toward me, then thinks better of it and stops. Every line of his body pulls taut, his stillness so profound that it gives the impression he's trembling. "Asked. What?"

The moment holds, pivoting around that question. But I won't repeat myself. I *can't*. This represents an overture neither of us has made before, and he has to give me something. I can't bridge this gap on my own.

At my silence, Weston rakes a hand through his sweat-dampened blond hair. His eyes drop to the line of red at my wrist before snapping back up.

Without a word, he retrieves a rag and a brown glass bottle

of antiseptic from a shelf. He sets them on the desk and pushes them toward me, then snatches his fingers back the second I reach out.

His withdrawal hurts. It shouldn't, but it does, and before my grip can close around the bottle, I pause. I can't seem to muster the courage to ask for what I want, but I can't just walk away. Because this is it. Our last chance.

After a moment's hesitation, I extend my arm, exposing the jutting splinter. "You do it."

"What?" Weston's eyes flare. "No. I can't."

I step closer. He flinches but doesn't back up, just levels me with his usual intensity, the kind that makes the air boil in my lungs. This close, his face is a collection of sharp angles, his eyes the color of a sunbeam slanting through honey.

Except, no, nothing about Weston is sweet. Better compare those eyes to whiskey—to that priceless bottle stored on the highest shelf, the one I never should've taken down, because now that I've suffered its bite, I can't stop drinking.

"Don't ask me that, Birdie," he murmurs. All the anger from a moment ago bleeds out of him, leaving him hoarse. "One touch, and I'd strip you of your luck. Forever. You know that."

"And I'd strip you of yours," I say, just as quietly. "Don't act like that would be a bad thing."

"It would, for you."

"But not for you."

He chokes down a swallow before his attention drifts to my mouth. And I feel it—the familiar thickening that coils between us, that rope of heat that binds us together. It's real, isn't it? It has to be. So is the rawness of this moment, because when we stand close like this, I'm just a woman. He's just a man. The Charm and the Null have faded, leaving two ordinary people.

"What're you asking me?" he whispers.

"To..." I gulp down the raw burn scalding my throat. Now or never. Fortuna help me. "...touch me."

His brows pinch and his eyes slam closed. When he opens them again, his expression suggests I've just rammed a knife into his gut.

"Curses," he says. "You know I can't."

"You can."

"No. I *can't*. For so many reasons. One being that I made your brother a promise, before I even met you. I swore I'd never touch you, no matter what happened. It was the only way Brendan would bring a Null home to meet a Charm, and I've made sure he's never regretted trusting me."

My brother's name slinks through the shadowy office like an intruder. "It's not his decision, though," I say. "It's mine. My Mark. To keep or give away as I choose."

A reluctant heat creeps into Weston's gaze, tempering the hard line of his jaw. On the surface, we're discussing him tending to my injury. But this conversation is actually about something else.

"I know. But..." His voice dips. "Brendan isn't the only person I promised. I promised *myself*. I swore I'd never take your magic. Even if, in some moment of misguided charity, you actually offered it to me."

Something inside my chest splinters and breaks. This isn't charity. It's something bigger. Something deep and wide and *right*.

Except I'm the only one who recognizes that, apparently.

"I'm not worthy of it." Weston's voice hardens as he steps

back. He pulls at the linen strips that encase his hands. They fall away, exposing swollen, battered knuckles. Bruises and scrapes mar the tanned expanse of his chest. "I mean, look at me. I'm no one. Nothing. Cursed."

I take him in, certain I've never seen anything more magnificent. Because under that topography of muscle and bone beats the heart of a gentleman—an eternally angry one, maybe, but a man of honor. And behind those golden eyes spins a mind that soaks up numbers just as readily as words.

Weston is...everything. The complete package. Every last thing I've ever wanted, all in one place.

"I don't think of you as cursed," I say.

His brows crook. "You should. You have to. Because it's the reason I can't let you waste yourself on me. Don't you understand? I have nothing to give. Fortuna made sure I can only take. Especially when it comes to you."

A sting pricks my eyes. I shake my arm, displaying the bloodied splinter. Weston's eyes follow the motion reluctantly.

"Will you just touch me?" I say, half-choked. "Please?"

Then none of this will matter. The circumstances of our births will cease to mean anything. All he has to do is reach out.

Pain carves lines across his brow. "Why? Why would you even ask me that?"

"Because. I..." The truth burbles in my throat, then snags on my tongue. *I love you. I want to be your wife.*

"Do you pity me?" he says. "Is that what this is about?"

"No, I... It's..." Frustration locks my teeth together. I can't say it. Why can't I say it? "Just let me give you this."

He scans me, then turns away, his jaw tensing, his shoulders drawn up.

"No," he says, and walks out, leaving me to clean and bandage my injury on my own.

Or one of them, at least.

The scar he's just carved into my heart won't heal any time soon.

Chapter Four

That night, after I cry myself to sleep, I dream of the woman in the market. The one I met when I was eleven.

My dream plays out exactly the way it happened.

It's the first day of spring. Blue shadows layer the market square while icicles drip toward nonexistence, a steady dribble against the cobblestones. Half of Pine's End browses in the newfound sunshine. The scent of roast mutton warms the air.

I'm trailing Brendan through the market, aimlessly enjoying the tender kiss of spring, when I spot the woman.

I stop in my tracks. It's rare enough to encounter a stranger in Pine's End—this town would barely exist if not for the cotton mill—but that's not what has me frozen.

The woman is Marked. A black triquetra peeks through the ties of her cloak, but where my tattoo looks like a crown, hers is inverted. Its downward-facing point resembles a falling teardrop rather than the upthrust jewel of a diadem.

She's...a Null.

My jaw slackens. I've never seen one of my counterparts before. They're just as rare as Charms, and most don't display the evidence of their curse so openly. They don't show off their Marks, the way my parents insist I do.

Beside me, a woman with a toddler stops to pluck something off the cobblestones. "Would you look at that?" Pleasure thickens her voice. "Someone dropped an entire gold piece. What're the chances?"

I barely register her pocketing of the coin. The chill nips at my bare throat as I start forward.

The Null doesn't notice my approach. She stands at a tented stall, inspecting a bolt of sapphire silk. When I'm halfway to her, a crack echoes though the crisp air. A block of snow breaks free atop the stall and slides down the canopy, then lands directly on her head. Slush drips from her forehead and nose.

I stare in horrified fascination. Nothing like that has ever happened to me before, but she doesn't look surprised. Something flashes in her eyes—embarrassment, maybe? She brushes the frozen chunks away, her movements sluggish with resignation.

The stall owner offers her a rag. He hesitates upon seeing her Mark, but she snatches the cloth, anyway, then hands it back when she's finished. Her dark brows carve a vee between her eyes as she hurries away.

I glance behind me. Brendan is distracted, haggling over a bar of soap, and I clutch my cloak closed to hide my Mark. I dart after the Null, intercepting her just as she ducks around a vegetable stand.

My free hand shoots out, clamping around hers. Bare skin to bare skin.

She turns to face me, puzzlement creasing her features. The crisp day—or maybe the snowball to the face—has coaxed color from her cheeks.

"What is it, sweetie?" she says. "Are you lost?"

My grip tightens. I don't know how long this is supposed to take. No one does, considering it's done so rarely. Some say a few seconds. Some say a few minutes. Some say it's different every time, depending on the Null and the Charm.

My parents have always insisted I never chance it at all.

But now a buzz hatches in my fingertips, the tremor of two opposing magics equalizing across the bridge of our skin.

A heartbeat later, the woman realizes what's happening. Her eyes widen. She tries to pull back, but I cling to her, reveling in the building tingle.

"Let go," she hisses. "What're you doing?"

"Don't you want me to?" I say, plaintive. Because I do.

I want to.

"Yes, of course, but...but...you're a *child*." Panic pitches her voice upward.

One heartbeat. Another. The world narrows, locking us into a moment of cosmic convergence. The thrum of the market fades, until nothing remains but the accelerating hum of our joined hands.

A heady sense of release overtakes me. My luck is dying. Bleeding out. In another moment, there will be no more rules. No more being paraded around. No strangers clamoring to get near me, no stares glued to my chest as though I were born without a face.

The woman searches me with bewildered eyes. "Stop," she says, and this time she yanks. Hard.

A pair of large hands clamps down on my shoulders,

wrenching me backwards. The connection severs. A burst of magic crackles across my skin.

"Bria!" Brendan's voice is thunder in my ears. He grips me by the shoulders and shakes me. "What're you doing?"

I gape at him as spots burst in my vision and fade. For a moment, I wonder how he found me. Shouldn't my luck have prevented it? But then my glance falls on the Null. She stands unmoving, a fist pressed to her belly. She's still plenty close enough to cancel my luck.

Right.

Brendan has gone pale. "You can't touch her, she's cursed. What were you even thinking?"

A sob swells in my chest. The woman's Mark is still there, which means mine is, too. But I cage my reaction with a swallow. "I'm sorry," I lie. "I just...lost track of you. I was going to ask if she'd seen a boy with brown hair. I didn't realize. I didn't see her Mark."

The Null woman fixes me with a piercing stare, and I beg with my eyes. *Please don't tell.*

"Okay." Brendan's breath rushes out of him. "Okay, it was just an accident. But we need gloves. You have to wear gloves, so there are never any mistakes."

"Yes," I say, like the pliant, dutiful sister I am. "No mistakes."

The Null watches as Brendan leads me away. The bustle of Pine's End reasserts itself, and soon I'm awash in the hustle of vendors, the clatter of mule carts, the fragrant waft of cinnamon.

But a dull ache drags at me. I was *so* close. For one vivid, shining moment, I was almost normal.

When we reach the edge of the square, Brendan unlaces

my cloak, then studies my triquetra as if counting each point. "Mom and Dad would've killed me," he mutters. "You *have* to be more careful."

"Right," I say. "Careful. I will be."

The memory—or dream—shifts and dissolves, releasing me into wakefulness. I open my eyes and blink up at the ornate canopy over my bed. A wash of gray light filters through the curtains.

Shame smolders in my belly. I sit up in the predawn and run my hands through my long brown waves. Fortuna help me, I hate that dream. I hate remembering what I did to that woman. I hate knowing I almost took away her choice.

I may have been a child, but that's no excuse. Regret set in even before Brendan pulled me through the doors of our gigantic, unearned house that day, pleading with me not to tell our parents what he'd almost let happen.

I swore I wouldn't.

I also swore—privately—never to do to anyone else what I nearly did to that Null. Never again would I treat someone as their Mark. As a means to an end. I, of all people, should know better.

Which is why, in ten years, I've never touched Weston, never grabbed onto him by "accident." Why it would've had to be his choice.

At the thought, my chest twists, and I flop down again, giving the window my back. I should probably get more sleep. But when I close my eyes, only jagged pain awaits. Someone has hacked a decade's worth of hope out of my skeleton and left a ragged, dripping wound behind. The agony of it steals my breath.

Is this what normality feels like? Maybe. Most unMarked

people have probably, at some point in their lives, wanted a thing so badly it's fused with their soul, only to have it wrested away.

Maybe I'm not cut out for that, after all.

I stay in bed, but sleep eludes me. Today, my brother will sell me to the highest bidder. He'll ensure my luck provides our family with yet another infusion of riches, and our parents will probably celebrate by extending the trip they jaunted off on six months ago. They'll gallivant around the continent for another year or three, and I'll spend my days making superficial conversation with Calder or Bastian or Theodore. At night, in bed, I'll turn my gaze away. Stare at the wall until they've finished.

I burrow deeper into the sheets. I don't actually care who it ends up being. Their faces blur together in my mind, a hazy composite of every man that isn't Weston.

There may be ninety-nine choices, but to me, they're all the same.

At least, that's what I go into Brendan's office believing, when I drag myself up to the third floor, two hours later. My attendant, Minnie, has dressed and brushed me and laced my corset tight enough to pinch.

Which I don't mind, today. It distracts from the serrated pain in my heart.

Brendan looks up from the papers he's perusing. Excitement glows in his face.

"What?" I say, wary.

"You'll never believe it." He can barely contain his grin. "We've had a hundredth proposal. Just this morning."

My pulse stutters. "What? From who?" I try and fail to mask the hope in my voice.

"Well, as luck would have it..." Brendan pauses, seemingly for dramatic effect. "The duke of Alverton. He's offered a fortune for you. And not a small one."

The light flickering within me abruptly gutters out. The duke of Alverton. The duke of *Alverton?* No, he's a cutthroat shark of a businessman, twice widowed and with a reputation for being just as ruthless with his wives as his investment partners.

I don't even question those rumors, because my mother used to invite the late duchess to tea. Even as a child, I under-stood that something terrible had befallen that woman. She cringed at the faintest sound. She only spoke when addressed directly. Every time I saw her, she reminded me of a horse whose spirit had been broken.

I'd sooner hurl myself from a third-story window than be shackled to the duke of Alverton.

"No," I say. "Absolutely not. Anyone but him."

Brendan frowns. "Lower your voice, will you? He's come all the way from the country. He's downstairs right now, waiting for my answer. Waiting for my *agreement*."

Each word drives another stake through my heart. I grope for a nearby chairback to prop myself up.

This can't be happening. My luck should prevent the duke from even *thinking* of offering for me. I glance down at my chest, half expecting to find it bare, but my triquetra stares back, a mocking black gleam in the early light.

"Impossible," I whisper.

Brendan's frown deepens. "It's not. Which says something, doesn't it? Your luck wouldn't let me pair you with someone you wouldn't like. Which means you'll probably fall in love with him. You'll probably be deliriously happy. You'll have a dozen strapping sons."

The floor tilts, the room receding. Fortuna, I don't want a dozen sons. I can't stand the thought of being kept, of being milked for my luck and forced to bear children for a man old enough to be my father.

I want...

Panic squeezes me until my fingertips tingle. Out. I want out. I need to run.

I stumble backward, then turn on my heel and flee. Bitter tears sting my eyes. The hallway rushes past, then the staircase, then another. I barrel down the final step and crash into a solid body. I reel back, peering up at a face I've never seen before.

My insides liquify. He's...handsome. Older, yes, but the years have carved a rugged symmetry into his features, the kind only men get to enjoy. A few silver streaks thread hair the color of iron. His waistcoat is cut from rich red brocade, the shirt beneath as spotless as freshly milled paper.

He smiles. "Bria Radcliffe, I presume?"

My throat works, but nothing emerges.

His eyes trail over my hair and face, ultimately landing on my Mark. His sapphire eyes glint. "Very pretty."

I don't know if he means me or my tattoo. Nor do I care. I try to push past him, but he catches me by the arm, spinning me around and backing me against the wall.

My thoughts ricochet inside my head like rubber marbles. He shouldn't be here. He shouldn't be able to offer for me, shouldn't be able to lay hands on me at all.

This is one stroke of bad luck after another, and it makes no sense.

The duke leans close. His proximity accelerates my breathing. A smile flickers across his mouth. "Not only pretty, but responsive, too, I see. That should make things less of a chore for me."

I whimper. Fortuna's blessings, how is this happening?

The duke grips my jaw and turns my head, inspecting me from this angle and that. I screw my eyes shut, but the wall prevents me from retreating. When I dare to look again, he's gazing at me with open avarice.

Or at my Mark, rather.

Movement flashes behind him. When I glance past his shoulder, silence fills my ears, a white roar that blots everything else out. It's...Weston. Standing in the foyer, not ten feet away. He looks stricken.

Suddenly, the situation makes sense. With him here, my luck might as well not exist.

"Birdie?" he says. My nickname drops into the quiet, small and misshapen.

I don't stop to consider. I just open my mouth. "Help. Help me. *Please*."

At my broken plea, Weston's brows lower, his uncertainty hardening into the surly look I know so well. He crosses the foyer in three long strides, then grabs the duke's shoulder and wrenches him away. "Get your hands off her."

Outrage twists the duke's features. He shakes off Weston's grip and looks him up and down. Then up again. He has no choice, considering Weston's height. "And who might you be?"

"A friend of the Radcliffes'." Weston throws his shoulders back. It's an obvious dare. A *hit-me-and-see-what-happens* challenge.

The duke barks out a derisive laugh. "A friend? Is that

35

right?" His gaze lingers on the worn fabric of Weston's shirt. "Well, whatever you are, you'd do well not to touch me."

Footsteps sound on the stairs, and Brendan appears. "*Weston?* What's going on? What're you doing down here?"

"That's what I'd like to know," the duke says hotly. "This...vagabond just saw fit to assault me."

"Because I asked him to," I cut in. "Because you laid hands on me."

Brendan shoots me a look clearly intended to silence me. "Alverton's your intended. It's not inappropriate for him to touch you."

Weston pales beneath his golden tan. "Intended? You're... No. You're marrying Bria to *him?*"

As the dust-storm of my panic settles, rational thought peeks through. Why does Weston sound so horrified? Does that mean he actually cares? And what is he doing in our foyer at eight o'clock in the morning? He must have a reason for showing up so early.

Which means maybe... Just maybe...

Hope flares in the dead canyon beneath my ribs. "Ask," I say.

Weston's attention swivels toward me. "What?"

"Ask." Desperation hurls words up my throat. "Please. For the love of Fortuna, just *ask*. I can't marry him."

Weston's eyes are pools of yellow fire, his focus so concentrated that it's like a hot poker tunneling through my skin. The moment looms, threatening to crush me beneath its weight.

But Weston ultimately straightens, his hands tightening into fists at his sides. His gaze swings to Brendan. "Let me marry Bria."

Air whooshes from my lungs. My entire being implodes into a cloud of glittering light.

I can't believe it. One hundred and one proposals. Thank the goddess, one hundred and one.

The duke is the first to recover, his laugh slashing across the quiet like a whip. "What? Don't be ridiculous, boy."

Brendan glares down at his best friend, his expression thunderous. "What did you just say?"

Weston raises his chin. "I said I'll marry her. Don't yoke her to this..." He surveys the duke as if contemplating someone far beneath his station. Which, really, he is.

"...brute," he finishes. "I can even make you an offer. Not as large as his, but I have some money. And I'll give Bria a home. I'll protect her. I'll give her my..." He trails off.

Tingles trail down my spine. I wait.

Weston swallows hard. "Everything. I'll give her everything. Even if we never touch."

A squeak flies from my throat. If I weren't leaning against the wall, I would crumple.

But Brendan's frown deepens. "What're you talking about? A Null can't marry a Charm. And my best friend can't marry my *sister*."

"Yes," I say. "Yes, yes, yes. I can." I don't even care about Weston's insistence on no touching. I'll convince him. I'll make him see.

"Double," the duke says.

I flinch. I'd almost forgotten him.

"What?" My brother's focus shifts.

The duke gives me a once-over and smiles. The sensation is like being slathered with rancid butter. "Now that I've seen her, I'll double my offer."

My brother goes rigid. A gleam sneaks into his eyes. One I recognize.

My heart swan dives into my feet. "Oh, no," I say. "No, please. I want Weston."

But Brendan isn't listening. He's *calculating*. I can see the numbers spinning behind his eyes, soaking into his mind. Poisoning him.

Our family doesn't need any more money, but that never stops my brother from wanting it. Now his decision takes even less time than I expect it to.

"You'll marry Alverton."

My next breath scorches my lungs raw. The duke says something, but I can't hear it over the catastrophic roar of my bones crumbling.

I anchor my palms to the wall. Any moment now, Fortuna will intervene. She has to. Except...

No. She isn't here. Not as long as Weston is.

"Why don't you come up?" Brendan says to the duke. "So we can iron out a contract?"

Alverton polishes his fingernails against his shirtfront, then follows my brother up the stairs, leaving Weston and me alone.

I struggle to breathe. I can't... Goddess, in all my daydreams, I never once imagined Weston proposing and being denied.

Which is stupid. I should have. I should've known Brendan would be blinded by a hefty enough price tag. I just assumed that things would all work out.

They always have before.

Weston stares at me, his brows crooked. My brother's refusal has gouged a wound into him—it's there in the way his shoulders sag, in the way his throat works around a painful-looking swallow.

A thousand unspoken words pass between us, but I can already tell it's a lost cause.

"Just take me," I plead. "Take me with you."

He shakes his head. "Birdie, I—"

My whimper cuts him off. "Don't tell me you can't. If you can marry me, you can steal me. Run away and take me with you. Just...don't let Brendan marry me to that horrible man."

He just stands there, looking as forsaken as I've ever seen him. "I don't have a choice," he says. "I'm not that lucky. Clearly. Even when I'm standing next to you. If I stole you, the duke would chase us. He'd *catch* us. You know that."

I gulp. I do know. Because wherever we went, as long as we were together, we wouldn't have my luck to shield us.

Weston turns away.

I want to cry out, to run after him, but my feet are rooted to the floor, nailed there by the weight of realization. He doesn't actually want me. He only made this gesture out of some misguided sense of nobility.

I want to throw up.

Weston pauses at the threshold, but he doesn't look back. A moment later, the door opens and closes. The enormity of what I've just lost crashes over me.

I slide down the wall. My one chance at freedom, at a life with the man I love...

Gone.

Chapter Five

For three days, I wander the halls like an automaton. I remind myself of a wind-up doll—I put one foot in front of the other, but there's no purpose behind it. No meaning. And sometimes, I simply wind down and stop. The world around me smears to a drab, quiet gray.

Meanwhile, the duke's dowry pours into my family's coffers. Trunks filled with gowns and jewels arrive, crowding the foyer.

Weston remains absent.

Which I should be grateful for, I know. Without him here, my luck can breathe. The cogs of fate can turn and align the balance in my favor. But he never goes this long without bringing me a book, and as the days slip past, I wonder if I'll ever see him again. Probably not.

I should be grateful for that, too. Because I know I have to forget him. Let him go. I've spent ten years pining for someone who doesn't want me back, and it's killing me.

So I push thoughts of Weston from my mind. I do my best to seal my hopeless longing into some hidden fold deep inside myself. I even consider going to Theodore again, like I did last year, when I gave up my virginity as much out of curiosity as desperation. I went knowing I couldn't touch Weston, but that I had to touch *someone*. That I deserved, just once, to know what it felt like to be wanted.

But I only ended up thinking of Weston the whole time, and I don't expect a second try to prove any different than the first. At least...not with Theodore.

So I stay home, and the days drag by. At times, I wonder if I imagined Weston's duty-bound proposal.

Maybe, because Brendan never mentions it. Nor does he waver in his decision to marry me to the duke. He insists that Fortuna wouldn't permit a match that wouldn't result in my happiness, and therefore I'll be utterly fulfilled as the new duchess of Alverton.

Every time he says it, I will myself not to gag.

I don't argue, though. I hunker down. I bide my time and wait for my luck to save me. It always has before.

Yet Fortuna fails to intervene, and a week after my forced engagement, I find myself being laced into my wedding dress by Minnie's capable hands. The gown has so many ruffles that a family of small animals could probably make a home in its skirts.

"Just your luck that this fits so perfectly," she says, tugging at the laces. "Considering the duke sent it without having your measurements taken."

I meet my own eyes in the floor-length mirror. There's no expression on my face. Not a single flicker of emotion. I can't seem to locate any within myself, either. "Yes. Lucky."

"Almost like this was meant to be," she continues. "Which, since it's you, I suppose it was."

She runs a brush through my hair and smiles at me in the glass. I try to smile back, but it ends up looking as though someone has knocked my mouth out of alignment.

"You had a hundred proposals, too," she says brightly. "Imagine that."

"A hundred and one, actually," I murmur.

Minnie pauses her brushing. "What?"

An eon passes.

I swallow hard. "Nothing."

Before I know it, she's leading me down the stairs. Brendan waits below, all smiles. He escorts me out front, to where the duke's garish carriage awaits. Twelve miles separate me from my fiance's country estate, but I wish it were twelve thousand.

Even that wouldn't be enough.

My brother wraps me in a hug. I stand there, feeling strangely boneless, and pray for Fortuna to show her hand. Any moment now, a crack of lightning will detonate inside my brother's mind. He'll tell me this is all an elaborate jest, that I don't have to marry at all. That we don't need any more money or riches, not at the cost of my happiness.

But when Brendan pulls back, he only says, "Are you sure you don't want me to come?"

I force a mute nod. A private ceremony is the one thing I managed to ask for. I can't tolerate the thought of anyone watching while I swear my life away. Or of Brendan being there to interfere when Fortuna finally executes whatever plan she has in mind.

Goddess, please let her have a plan in mind. Please.

Brendan urges me into the carriage. Minnie bursts into

tears and waves with both hands. I stare leadenly through the window as the door of my cage clicks shut.

The carriage lurches. At the first jostle of the wheels, sweat breaks out on my palms. This is...happening. Actually happening. I'm being delivered into my own worst nightmare, because once I reach my destination, I'll be married. Immediately. Tonight.

Come tomorrow, I'll be smothered in jewels. Entombed in silks. I'll spend my days as an ornament. As a conduit for the duke to leverage his fortune to even greater heights.

I stare at the fields zipping past, unable to fathom that future. Maybe an axle will snap. A stampede of wild animals will spook the horses and send us back the way we've come.

Something. *Anything.*

Then a few miles later, I see him—a blond rider, outlined against the ridge ahead. He tracks the carriage's progress with unsettling focus.

There's something about the way he sits atop his black horse. A...stillness, almost. An anticipation.

I squint. We draw close enough that I can make him out.

I don't recognize him. Broad features make up a face that's pleasant enough, but would prove easily forgettable if not for the way he measures our approach.

I press my face to the glass. The stranger meets my eyes and winks.

The carriage whips past.

I frown, craning my head as we hurtle onward, but I've lost sight of him. What was that about?

As if in answer, the pounding of hoofbeats joins the clattering of our wheels. When the sound grows louder—*closer*—my pulse quickens.

Someone shouts outside. Suddenly, the whole vehicle swerves. I'm thrown across the bench seat as something thunders past the window—that same rider, only now he's pulled a cloth mask down over his face. Wind plasters his golden hair to his forehead as he extends a gloved hand.

My blood roars in my ears. From this angle, I can't tell what he's reaching for, but he's clearly a criminal. A highwayman.

We're being robbed.

Somewhere overhead, the driver lets out a strangled cry. The carriage jounces as a weight tears free. Something heavy hits the ground with a nauseating crunch.

I scramble toward the window again, shoving the lace aside. The driver tumbles through the roadside grass behind us. When he comes to a stop, the man jumps to his feet and shakes a fist, but he's already shrinking to a speck. The black horse comes into view, now riderless.

My stomach clenches. The carriage bounces over one bump after another, and I cast a glance toward the ceiling. The highwayman must be driving, now.

I bang the roof with a fist but receive no reply. I try again, then sink onto the seat, my mind spinning. I can't leap out at this speed. Not without breaking something. With my luck, it'd likely be a non-essential something, but I have no desire to test the limits.

Half an hour spins by. The sun dips below the horizon. A few times, we change direction, careening around one corner or another. Finally, we veer off the main road and down a dirt track, into a jumble of grasping brambles. Each jolt threatens to expel the contents of my stomach.

We finally grind to a halt in a secluded hollow. The carriage creaks and settles.

Quiet descends. Nothing moves, save for the lace curtains. They swing in the waning light, then go still.

My heart convulses. Should I...get out? Stay here? Shout to the plain-faced highwayman to return me home?

Before I can decide, the carriage jostles. Footsteps crunch through the brush, and my lungs shrink. But this man won't hurt me, I tell myself. He'll take one look inside, realize I'm an innocent bride, and let me go.

With any luck, at least.

Heavy boots mount the footplate. I cower, having nowhere to hide, as the door wrenches open.

The highwayman fills the entryway, silhouetted by the crimson glow of dusk. He's swathed entirely in black—black boots, billowing black shirt, black cloth mask. Black leather gloves encase his hands.

I squint. I can't make out much else. Just a fall of blond hair and a muscular frame.

"Hello." His voice is low and gravelly. "Don't worry. You're not in any danger."

I search for words. I can barely locate any over the frenzy of my pulse. "That's a relief," I finally say.

He steps inside. I scramble to my feet, not wanting him towering over me, but he does, anyway. Fortuna, he's tall. And broad.

"I'm Jack," he says.

"Jack." I file the name away. "Okay. I'm Bri—"

"I know who you are."

I fall silent. His voice is scarcely more than a rumble, and it seems to saturate the air before settling into the lavish seats and priceless curtains. But I suppose it makes sense that he knows who I am. This carriage, and the triquetra staring him in the face, kind of give it away.

"What do you want with me?" I manage.

He doesn't answer right away. His expression might change, but the light from the doorway glares too brightly to tell.

"Are you ransoming me?" I prompt. If he knows I'm a Charm and came after me on purpose... "To the duke? Is this about money?"

"No," he says. "No, I...need you."

I blink.

"Your help." He clears his throat. It sounds like rocks grinding together. "I need your help. Your luck."

Surprise ripples through me. "My luck? For what?"

"It'd be easiest to just show you. It's close by. And this...purpose I need you for, it might take a while. So you won't be making it to the altar. Not today, at least."

"You're kidnapping me, then?" The words spill out, my voice trembling with disbelief. Disbelief and...something else.

Jack studies me through the dim light. "I guess you could call it that, yes. But you'll be safe. You'll be taken care of. I'll make sure of it."

"Oh." I press a hand to my chest. An undercurrent of conviction runs beneath his words, so palpable that I actually believe him. "Well, then."

"No harm will come to you," he insists.

My hand falls to my side. All the emotions of the last few days—the dread, the doubt, the agonizing helplessness—come undone at once. They unspool together, into a tangled heap at my feet.

In their wake, gratitude blossoms, so intense that tears prick at my eyes. Stolen. I'm being stolen. From my own wedding. I'm being *freed*.

Jack watches me, perhaps waiting for hysterics that never come.

In the next moment, my fear drops away. I sweep my gaze over him and see not a criminal, but my salvation.

Someone is finally stepping in where Weston and Brendan wouldn't. Someone is saving me. Someone hand-delivered by Fortuna herself.

My guardian angel.

"Kidnapped," I say. "Oh, thank the goddess. Or, more accurately, thank *you*."

The relief coursing through me intensifies, demanding some kind of outlet, and before I can think, I step in and press my lips to his.

Chapter Six

I intend the kiss to be quick. Just a simple peck to express my gratitude.

But the moment our mouths connect, Jack stiffens. His gloved hands rise to my waist and hover, as if he's warring with himself over how to respond.

As if he intends to push me away at any second.

Except...he doesn't push me away, and he feels good. Surprisingly so. His lips are warm and plush, molding to mine in a way that wakens my spent nerves.

A whole second sneaks by. Then another. And while Jack doesn't open his mouth, his stiffness yields a degree. Almost like a welcome. And Fortuna, how I've longed to feel a man's mouth on mine again. After Theodore, I tried so hard to hold out for the one I wanted. I hoped and hoped and hoped. But this small touch, this moment of connection, amounts to more than Weston was willing to give me.

Jack's posture softens. An unfamiliar heat spins into me, clouding my thoughts, and I forget to pull back.

And then something...happens.

Jack's hands settle around my waist, his thumbs clamping against my ribs. Then his hesitation shatters, all at once. He slants his head and pulls me flush against his body. The hard planes of his chest crush the air from my lungs.

And he kisses me. *Really* kisses me.

And...

Oh.

Sweet Fortuna. He does it incredibly well.

My body lights up, new pathways igniting along every nerve. My stomach tilts, tipping me toward some fiery precipice I didn't even know existed.

Jack makes a noise deep in his chest. It's not a moan or a groan, but something greater. Something starved. It's a miles-long yearning, compressed into sound.

That, more than anything else, makes me come undone.

Logic deserts me. I don't pause to watch it go. Our exchange turns ravenous, Jack's tongue parting my lips and plunging inside. He maps my mouth as his hand rises to cradle the back of my head, and the searing heat of it pulls me up on tiptoes. I fist my hands in the softness of his shirt, trying to anchor myself, but I'm lost. Adrift in the satin thrust of his tongue.

Instinct demands I press the length of my body to his. Jack responds by walking me backward until the backs of my knees meet the plush carriage bench. Then he's lowering me, his solid weight settling against me, one hand pillowed beneath my head as the other skims down my body. I hoist my legs up around his hips. A hungry rumble tears from his chest as he deepens the kiss, and I answer with the wanton moan climbing from my throat.

My skirts ride up. Our position is downright indecent, but it doesn't matter, absolutely nothing matters except the way this man kisses. It's like a storm is breaking inside him. Like we're falling into a bottomless abyss and I have no desire to resurface.

It's like he actually *wants* me.

I shudder, arching against the delicious friction of his hips grinding into mine. Goddess help me, I've never been kissed like this. Not by Theodore, not by anyone. I've only ever experienced anything this unchecked in my most private, aching dreams.

Then I feel it. What begins as a tingle in my tongue spreads outward, a hum that sets my nerves abuzz. At first, the sensation blends with the layers of intensity detonating inside me. Except this part...this is familiar.

I've felt it before.

My eyes pop open. Jack must notice something amiss, too, because his lashes whip apart. His mouth releases mine, all at once, and he rears back an inch.

Energy crackles as our lips part.

Silence crowds the carriage. My chest rises and falls. His does, too, his breath no more than a ragged tumult. His enormous body molds to mine in a way that lets me know he is very, *very* turned-on by this.

"Shit," he says. Shadows lance across his face, but I can still track his gaze as it races over my skin. But we aren't touching anymore, not with all this black fabric in the way.

I unwrap my arms from his broad back—slowly, so as not to spook him—and slide my hands into the scant inches between us. His shirt laces at the neck, so I ease the tie through the eyelets and pull the thing open.

Then I stare. Stare some more. There's just enough light left to confirm.

My eyes lift to his. Our gusted exhales entwine.

"You're a Null," I say.

Chapter Seven

Jack drops me onto the bench seat and rockets away like I've burned him.

"Wait," I say. "Where're you—"

"I'm sorry," he pants, and then he's flinging himself through the carriage door, yanking it shut behind him. He just...leaves me there, flat on my back, my skirts hiked up around my hips. Quiet flames pulse beneath my skin.

I stare at the ceiling. What the hell just happened? Never mind that a man has never touched me like that—how did I not know there's another Null in Pine's End?

Questions swarm me, so rapidly I can't make sense of them. I eventually straighten my skirts and right myself, then smooth down my hair with shaking hands. When I open the carriage door, Jack stands across the clearing, his back turned. He's little more than a black blot amid umber shadows, but his stance is filled with so much regret that I can't miss it, even in the dark.

"I'm sorry." His gruff baritone captures a wealth of feeling.

He turns his head, though not enough to look at me. "I don't know what happened."

A beat passes. "I kissed you," I say. "Which you were...not averse to, apparently."

His back flexes, his shoulder blades flaring like wings. He doesn't answer.

I step down from the carriage, careful not to catch my wedding dress on the footplate and go tumbling face-first onto the ground. With a Null standing fifteen feet away, it's a distinct possibility. "And I...didn't exactly hate it, either. Actually, if you really want to know, that was the most—"

"I don't."

The desperation in his voice shuts me up. "What?"

"I don't. Want to know. That's not what I'm here for." He sounds almost frantic. "I shouldn't be kissing you, or touching you, or getting anywhere near you. I shouldn't even be *looking* at you. I just need your help, and once that's done, I'll deliver you back to your life. *With* your Mark intact."

My blood cools. Silence piles between us. "Oh," I finally say.

"Fortuna's curses, I'm so incredibly sorry. And thank you. For coming to your senses. Before it would've been too late. I... Goddess, I have no excuse. I just..." He buries his face in his hands and releases a shuddering breath.

I wait, but he doesn't seem inclined to continue, so I glance around. Shadows lie thick in the clearing. Off to the right, a smudge of light glows through the trees. It might be a lantern, or a candle in a window.

"It's fine," I say.

He grunts a denial, clearly having no idea of just how much I mean that.

I rub at my arms. "Maybe you should show me what you need help with?"

Jack takes a measured breath and pivots. "Right. Yes."

He's a man of few words, I decide, because he unharnesses the horses and turns them loose in silence. He takes my trunk down from the carriage like it weighs nothing, then inclines his head to indicate I make my way into the trees.

I can't see much, but I follow the beckoning light, since there don't seem to be any other options. Pine branches snag my hems, and I wonder where we are. Probably halfway between my estate and the duke's, if I had to guess. Ten or so miles from Pine's End.

Not that it matters. We're ranged too far into the woods for me to run, though I wouldn't have, anyway. I have nothing to go back to, at the moment. Nothing besides misery and servitude.

The distant light brightens. We emerge into a clearing rimmed by shadowy bracken, where a stone-walled cabin awaits, tidy and adorable. A candle glows in one window, burned almost all the way down. Two doors occupy opposite ends of the building, while the shingled roof looks to be in good repair.

Jack motions me toward the left-hand entrance.

I make my way over and hold the door for him, seeing as how he's lugging my trunk. He grunts in acknowledgment, then edges around me in a way that inspires me to sniff at my armpits.

I don't smell, though. At least not that I can tell.

Inside, Jack sets my trunk at the foot of a bed that looks sturdy and inviting, if simple. The white bedding gleams in the light of the sentinel candle.

SHAYLIN GANDHI

I take the place in. A quaint table and two chairs occupy the space by the window, opposite a corner hearth that looks remarkably pristine. A generous bookshelf sits against the wall, almost comically large, because the room proves far smaller than expected. The cabin's exterior isn't exactly grandiose, but it didn't suggest *this* level of coziness, either. Then I realize.

"The door," I say.

Jack takes my measure. I wish I could determine his eye color, but in the candlelight, everything takes on the same wan shade of gold. "What about it?" he says.

"The *other* door, I mean. Where is it?"

Something flickers across what little I can see of his face. It might be appreciation, or simply a trick of the light. Or of the mask. "There're two sides," he says. "They don't connect."

"Oh." I do another sweep of the room. It's cute. Clean. How strange that it's walled off from the other half. "And what do you need my help with, exactly? Not keeping house, from what I can tell."

"No." His jaw flexes. "There's a woman. In the other room. She took ill a few weeks ago with the flu, and it's taken a turn. A bad one. She doesn't have much hope at the moment, but I'm hoping you can fix that."

I blink. "She got the flu in *September*?"

His shoulders tighten. "Back in August, actually. She'd been...spending time with me. So." Coldness coats his gravelly words.

I press my lips together, not needing him to elaborate. Clearly, he blames himself—and his ill-fated luck—for this woman's condition.

Then my thoughts hit a snag and go tumbling. "Wait. This woman...she's not your wife, is she?"

Nausea snakes up my throat. Did I just force a married man into an out-of-control make-out session? Did I betray this poor woman while she's dy—

"No." Jack bites the word off clean at the end. "I'd never inflict myself on anyone in that capacity. So...no. You don't have to worry about that."

Relief washes through me, muddled with dismay that he thinks of himself as something that can be *inflicted*. "Oh. Okay."

He waves a gloved hand as if to brush aside this line of questioning. "The point is, I need you to stay here for a little while. In this room, close enough that she can soak up your luck. So she can beat the odds and get better. Please."

I nod along. "That's it?"

"That's it. I'll bring you meals every evening. And anything else you need. Once she recovers, you can go..."

Home, my mind supplies. Only nothing about the word entices me. Brendan will only send me back to the duke.

"...wherever you want," he finishes.

I clear my throat. Wherever I want.

Really, if I had my way, I'd stay lost. I'd sooner lie in bed and read all these books—which are so numerous the shelves sag in the middle—than see the duke again. Much less endure his touch. "Okay. That doesn't sound so bad. But where will you be? While this is happening?" Not here, clearly. If Jack sticks too close, he'll nullify my luck and leave his...whoever she is...unprotected.

He inclines his head toward the window. "Out there."

I frown. "In the woods?"

"I'll sleep just far enough away for your luck to work. But not so far that you should consider running."

"I wouldn't," I say, a tad crisply. "If a life needs saving, of course I'll do it. You didn't even have to kidnap me. You could've just stopped the carriage and asked. I would've gladly come with you."

"The duke's man would never have let you go. So yes. I did have to kidnap you."

Silence descends as I absorb that, because he's right. On the far side of the wall, bedsprings creak, followed by someone coughing. It's deep and hacking and sounds like it's tearing their lungs apart.

I wince. So does Jack. As if reminded of his purpose, he breaks away and goes to the fireplace. He kneels and fiddles with some kindling in silence.

I rub at my bare arms again, trying to generate some heat. Now that night has fallen, it's getting chilly. The countryside around Pine's End is often like this in early September—comfortable during the day, nippy at night. And yet the fireplace looks immaculate. As if no one has used it in a while.

While Jack works, I wander toward the bed and sit. The mattress feels every bit as welcoming as it looks. "That's the cleanest hearth I've ever seen. Do you not stay here, usually?"

Jack grunts. It's not a friendly sound, but it's not exactly unfriendly, either. How strange to think that, just minutes ago, I had his tongue in my mouth. Had the hard length of him pressed against my core.

"I live here," he says. "Away from... Well. Away. But I don't usually use the fireplace. Something always goes wrong. The chimney clogs and smokes up the whole cabin, or a freak gust blows sparks through the room. One time a hawk flew overhead and dropped a rabbit down the chimney. It wasn't alive anymore, but...it still made a mess. Fur and embers everywhere."

His gaze strays to a mark on the floor, barely visible in the budding firelight. A patch the size of my palm has been charred into the plank.

"I learned my lesson after that," he rumbles. "But with you here, it should be fine."

A pang circles my heart, then pulls tight. I've known. Ever since meeting Weston, I've understood that while I sail through life, Nulls meet with struggle after struggle. And at times, I've come within spitting distance of cursing Fortuna, because I don't understand why the goddess would give to her flock with one hand while taking with the other. It seems...spiteful. Petty.

Yet something about the naked resignation in Jack's voice accesses a whole new level within me, some basement horizon that opens onto regret.

"I'm sorry," I say. "That you've had to deal with that your whole life. It's...not fair. I'll never understand it, honestly. Why Fortuna does this to us."

He pauses and looks at me.

I gnaw at my lip. Nulls and Charms probably don't typically discuss this. Even Weston and I always avoided the subject, though I couldn't say exactly why.

"You don't like being a Charm?" he finally says. A note of wariness threads his tone.

I consider. The answer to that question is one I've never admitted to anyone. The closest I've ever come was with that Null woman in the marketplace, when I was eleven.

But something about this stranger, this anonymous highwayman in his black mask, frees my tongue. He could be anyone. I could be anywhere, talking to the sky or the woods or simply myself.

"I hate it," I say.

Jack drops the log he's holding. I swear it happens more slowly than gravity should allow. The wood hits the hearth with a hollow thunk. "How's that possible?"

Low flames crackle behind him. I'm glad I can't really see him. It's easier to confess to a shadow. "Because," I say. "People have always treated me like I'm...this." I wave to indicate my Mark, trusting he'll know what I mean. If anyone will, it's him.

"But everyone worships you," he says slowly.

"No." I scoff. "They worship the tattoo. They worship what it means. What it can give them."

He swivels to his task again, but I get the sense that he's thinking. Hard.

My heartbeat swells to occupy the quiet. I have no idea why I just told him that, but having done so unspools something kept tightly caged within my ribs.

Jack feeds the fire until the glow brightens. I relax against the pillows and watch him work, lulled by the shift of muscle beneath fabric. Once the flames gain a foothold, he rises.

"I think I get it." His words are tinged with something like bitterness. "But for me, people treating me like my Mark has always come as a relief. It's...easier like that. Better not to have to push people away. Because I'm not always very good at it. Clearly."

My breath catches. "That sounds lonely." More accurately, it's cruel.

"What you're describing does, too." He runs a hand along

his jaw. "I've never stopped to think that all that adoration might seem...artificial."

A spark suffuses me. *Artificial.* That's the perfect word. Nothing about my life is organic, or natural. It's predetermined. Shaped by hands that aren't my own.

"There's more to it, too," I say. "Sometimes, I wonder what being Marked has done to me. What kind of person you become when life just hands everything over, without a fight."

The fire backlights him, obscuring his expression, but something in his stance shifts. "Probably the opposite kind of person you become when life refuses to give you a single thing you want."

Silence settles, but it doesn't feel awkward. It's dark and velvety, stuffed with meaning and stitched up with threads of kinship.

At least, that's how it feels to me. Because while Jack and I technically occupy opposite poles of luck's spectrum, I sense in his answer a ghost of the same powerlessness that lives in me.

Neither of us asked for this. Neither of us has any say.

At the thought, my fingers sneak to my lips. They feel swollen. Beautifully bruised.

Jack clears his throat and scrubs at the back of his neck. "I'd better not stand here all night," he says, clipped. "I should give your magic a chance to work. Do you need anything?"

My chest clenches at the thought of him bedding down in the woods. But I know he can't stay here, not if he wants his friend to recover. "I don't suppose you have any milk?"

"Milk?"

A blush stains my cheeks. "I know. I'm a grown woman,

and it's weird. But I've loved milk ever since I was a kid. I still have a glass every night. I swear it helps me sleep."

A beat passes. "I didn't say it was weird. And there's some in the coldbox. Outside."

I blink. That's...lucky.

"I just figured you'd need more than that. Isn't there anything else?"

"No. I'm pretty low maintenance."

His eyes wander over my lavish wedding dress, and my blush kicks up a notch.

"Despite appearances," I add.

He nods and makes for the door, but I can't quite bear for him to leave me alone. Not yet.

"You're a good kisser," I blurt. "Phenomenal, actually. That was—"

He stiffens as if shot. "Goodnight, Bria," he chokes out.

Before I can say more, he wrenches open the door and disappears into the night.

Chapter Eight

That night, I dream of Weston.

It's not a pleasant experience, like my usual nocturnal imaginings of him. This dream is raw and painful, brimming with accusation.

We're at the cotton mill, right back in Calder's office, only this time, Weston has me caged against the wall. He leans close, his hands planted to either side of my head.

"You kissed him," he hisses. "A man who *kidnapped* you. How could you? Don't I mean anything to you?"

It's something Weston would never say, and that alone tells me I'm dreaming. Which frees me to unleash the full brunt of my frustration.

"Of course you do," I snap. "You're all I ever wanted, you ridiculous ass. Which is exactly why I kissed Jack. Because I'm sick to death of you refusing to touch me, of wondering endlessly what you would feel like. I kissed him because I needed to do anything besides want and want and want you all the time. I kissed him because I needed to forget you."

Weston's lip curls. He's angry. That much, at least, is true to life. "I guess you're going to tell me that's why you kissed Theodore, too? Why you gave yourself to someone who isn't even worthy of hearing you breathe?"

"Of course I am." My chin rises, and he leans closer, as if magnetized. "I let Theodore take whatever he wanted from me, just so I could feel something. But you know what? I didn't think about him once. I tried, but all I could think about was someone else."

Weston's glare deepens, a lethal amber glint in the shadows. "Who? Who else?"

I glare right back. Fortuna, sometimes I just want to hit him. Most of the time, actually. "You already know."

His tongue slides over his bottom lip. "Maybe. Maybe I do. But you know I can't let you waste yourself on me."

My control frays, and I reach for him. The fact that he thinks of it that way, as a waste instead of a mutual gift, cracks my anger down the middle. But the meager distance proves uncrossable. It swells and swells, my fingers catching at empty air.

I can't let you waste yourself on me.

His words echo until I'm falling into them, and then I'm spiraling upward, pulled into awareness by the hack and scrape of someone fighting for breath.

My eyes flutter open. I startle at first, unsure of where I am, but then it all rushes back. I sit up. In the other room, someone is coughing themselves into oblivion.

I ease from bed, anchoring my hands to the wall, and pad along until I'm directly opposite the sound. I flatten my body to the stone, lending the poor woman as much of my lucky bubble as I can.

Her coughing dwindles. A few rattling breaths lance into her lungs, and she quiets. Sheets rustle.

I hope she's able to get comfortable.

"It's going to be okay," I say to the wall. "I'm going to make sure you get better."

If she hears me, she doesn't say anything. I stand there for what feels like an hour while the chilled rock pulls the warmth from my bones. Last night, I dug a nightgown out of my trunk—a gift from the duke, finely woven and softer than butter—but the silk proves too thin to insulate me.

When I start to shiver, I peel myself away and go to the fireplace.

The ashes should be long cold, considering dawn's light is peeking through the window and no one has fed the fire since last night.

But a tiny pocket of embers glows at the back. The moment I nudge it with a stick of kindling, flames burst to life.

I blink. Jack must not be nearby.

Within minutes, I have a crackling fire going. I hang a kettle of porridge over the flames and add a splash of the milk I brought in from the coldbox last night.

Then I stand before the merry fire and frown. There were *eight* bottles out there, and little else. Which, in any other circumstances, I would ascribe to my luck, but Jack shouldn't be affected by that. It's almost like he knew.

A thud jars me from my ruminations.

I glance around to find a book splayed on the floor, fallen from the bookcase. When I move closer, I see that it's my favorite. An adventure tale, about a woman who assumes a man's identity and joins a pirate crew, only to fall in love with every sailor aboard. She ultimately reveals her true self and sails off into a life of crime and passion, now the treasured darling of twenty gifted lovers.

It's utterly unrealistic, and I couldn't adore it more. But I haven't read it in years.

I pluck the book from the floor. Just my luck that a copy of this would find its way here.

I settle back into bed with my find. Within moments, I'm aboard the *Dolphin of the Dawn*, the sea breeze crisp in my face, my lashes stiff with salted spray. I'm so engrossed that I forget the porridge, but fortunately, a log cracks in the fireplace at the precise moment the kettle almost bubbles over. I leap to my feet and save my breakfast just in the nick of time.

Once I've filled my belly, I return to the book. I even shove the bedframe over a few feet so I can lie directly opposite the mystery woman. She coughs and tosses a few times, but I barely hear it, because now the heroine is mid-rendezvous with Charlie, the pirate captain who's uncovered her secret before anyone else. He's locked her in the captain's quarters, and the crew outside assumes that all that shrieking is because he's caught her stealing and is now punishing her.

That's definitely not what's happening.

The day slips by. I spend it on the high seas, and when I turn the last page, barely enough light slants through the window to see by.

I close the book and set it on the quilt. I can't believe I just spent an entire day inside. I can't believe I spent a day in *bed*. Reading.

Goddess, I love this place.

A chill is falling along with the dusk, and I rise to tend to the dwindling fire. I'd expected to see Jack again by now, but when I think about it, he did say he'd come in the evening.

I wonder why. Maybe he works. Maybe he was far away today, despite saying he'd stick close enough to ensure I didn't run.

The woman coughs again. I toss together a slapdash dinner—crusty brown bread from the cupboard and a few slices of cheese from the coldbox—and dive back into bed. The moment I do, my charge's struggle eases.

I lie there and listen to her bedsheets rustle. When everything quiets, my mind roams. Inevitably, my thoughts land on Weston.

That dream. In it, I told him everything I long to say, the same words that forever crowd my throat and never find air. Except what he said back to me—that was real. *I can't let you waste yourself on me.*

He spoke those exact words in Calder's office.

The memory gnaws at me, quiet and relentless. For the first time since he left me in my foyer, I consider that maybe Weston's hesitation about helping me is because of the threat he poses to my Mark. Well...that and the fact that my brother refused him. But if I wasn't a Charm anymore, Brendan would no longer have the option of marrying me to the duke. He'd have no choice but to accept another proposal, and Weston would have no reason to keep his distance any longer. We'd be on equal footing, then.

I sit up and cram the last of the sandwich into my mouth, my mind tilting into motion like a boulder tipping downhill.

Weston may have refused to take my luck, but he's not the only Null I can appeal to. There's another one, right here in my hands.

A smile itches at my lips. Maybe Fortuna had a plan in mind this whole time.

As if to confirm my suspicions, the door handle turns.

When Jack walks in, he finds me grinning from my place in bed. He wears the same ensemble as yesterday, right down to the black mask. The sun has set, and only a hint of peach light coaxes a sheen from the fabric. Shadows layer the rest of him.

"What?" he says, leery. "Why're you smiling like that?"

I rein in my expression. I probably look demented, grinning at my captor like I've never been so happy to see someone before.

But I *am* happy, because Jack is the answer. The solution to the thorny puzzle currently looped around my neck.

"No reason," I say. "Except that I missed you."

He draws a soft inhale. That might have been too much, but it's not actually a lie. And it paves the way for me to dare bigger, bolder things.

Because I intend to leave this cabin with more than just a wild story to tell. I'm going to go with a smooth expanse of unmarked skin between my collarbones.

So is Jack.

Chapter Nine

Jack carries the bag of food he's brought to the tiny kitchenette and sets it on the countertop. He avoids my eyes as if, in doing so, he can dodge what I just said. "Do you need anything else?" he says. "Besides milk?"

"Not that I can think of."

"Right." He spins and makes to leave. "Then I'll just—"

I leap from bed and intercept him, slotting myself between his hulking body and the door. He backs up, practically recoiling in his haste to get away from me.

My fingers flex at my sides, the tips tingling. What a strange feeling, to wield power over a man like this. He's tall and broad and solid, the proportions of his body alien beside mine, yet when I step toward him, his entire frame tenses as if to ward off my next move.

I sidle yet another step closer.

"What're you doing?" he says, his voice low and rasping.

Fortuna. I'm probably evil for doing this. For plotting.

But Jack will benefit from us touching just as much as I will. He can ride off into the sunset, curse-free, and I'll return to Pine's End Markless and magicless. Weston will have no reason to refuse me, then. I'll find out if any part of him has ever considered the idea of us.

I smile up at Jack. "Actually, I do need your help with something."

He swallows audibly. "With what, exactly?"

"My hair. It needs to be brushed and braided."

Silence pools between us. Again, I can't see his face, and I wonder if this is why he insisted on evenings—so he could hide from me, like he did yesterday.

"It's not like I can do it myself," I say. It's half true—Minnie always attended to my hair. Truth be told, I could probably manage on my own, but that's not the point. "If I let it go, it'll get all tangly and hopeless and I'll have to cut it off."

He flinches, like the idea of that pains him. An eternity slides past as he considers.

"It's just my hair," I add. "And you have gloves on."

"Fine," he finally says.

My tongue presses to the roof of my mouth, walling off the whoop that gathers in my throat. This will give us a chance to talk. To touch. Sort of.

"Great." I force my voice even. "Thank you."

He shifts his weight. "Where...?"

"Over by the fire."

He nods, or I think he does. The flames have died back, and it's hard to tell amid all these shadows.

I feel my way through the dimness and find my trunk, where I rummage for my sterling silver hairbrush. The thing is edged in gold and utterly ridiculous—plain wood would've worked just as well—but it's all I have.

At the fire, I toss on a few logs. Light leaps when the wood catches. Jack keeps to the shadows, as if waiting for me to turn my back before emerging into the light.

I shrug at his reticence, then settle on the floor in front of the paisley armchair that faces the fire. I wait. And wait.

Finally, heavy footfalls approach. The chair groans when Jack lowers his considerable weight. His black-clad knees appear in the edges of my vision, bracketing my body. I hold up the brush without glancing back.

He takes it, but doesn't seem to know where to start.

"You do know how to braid, right?" I prompt.

A pause. "In theory. But I've never actually done it before."

"Really? You've never had a woman ask? Never done it for one of your lovers?"

He makes a soft, strangled sound. I'm probably not supposed to bring up things like that so casually, but honestly, we're both adults. And this is nothing compared to the book I spent the day immersed in.

"No," he says. "The truth is, I always get away from them as quickly as possible. After I... Well. After."

I go still. Of course. He wouldn't want to stick around and burden anyone with his luck. He wouldn't want them catching the flu in August and nearly dying, just because they spent time in his proximity.

Once again, that fist of sympathy clamps around my heart. "Well, you don't have to worry about that with me. You realize that, right? I'm immune."

"I know."

The statement is sparse, and yet a world of meaning layers itself into the syllables. He sounds both desolate and relieved, and underneath it all, thankful to be sharing space with me.

To be freed for these few stolen moments from the burden of his curse.

I like it, too. Knowing I'm just a girl right now.

I draw up my knees and hug them close. Jack eventually lets go of a breath, so deep and prolonged it must empty his entire body of air.

He begins to brush.

He starts with the ends, just like Minnie always does, then works his way up. A few times, his gloved fingers brush against the nape of my neck. Each time, a shiver trills through my bones. Memories of our encounter in the carriage rise to the surface.

I let them flow. Ultimately, I might have to resort to kissing him again, because some internal directive took over for him in that moment, a hemmed-in hunger that broke loose and swallowed him whole. He was driven by pure need. I tasted it on his tongue.

Maybe I could reach that part of him again.

The brush rises and falls. I close my eyes, soothed by the swish of bristles, then by the gentle tug as he moves on to the plait. He's careful not to touch my scalp, despite his gloves, but it's something. A start.

And it feels incredible, really. There's something oddly intimate about letting a man do this, even if it's the unlikeliest of circumstances—me sitting by the fire in my nightgown, being attended to by my Null kidnapper.

When Jack finishes, he passes the brush back over my shoulder. I take it. I expect him to get up, but he doesn't, so I wait, my breath held.

After half an eternity, his hand grazes the back of my neck.

Or rather, his glove does. Leather glides against skin as he runs his thumb across my nape.

"It's lopsided," he says, and there's something wrong with his voice. Something strained. "The braid, I mean. Sorry."

I swivel around and look up.

His hand falls away. He stares down, his face swathed in shadow, the chair angled in such a way that the wingback casts him into darkness.

But I can see well enough to tell he doesn't spare a glance for my triquetra, even though my keyhole neckline offers the perfect viewing window. And the way he's looking at me…

"Thank you," I say.

Jack swallows, his throat a ripple of shadow and firelight. "You're welcome."

When he doesn't move, I rise up onto my knees. His breath catches in his throat. His gloved fingers curl into fists atop his thighs.

A heady tingle sheets through me. He seems so…affected by me. By this. And I'm not as immune as I'd like to be, because the moment writhes and sizzles. I never stare at people this intently, yet right now, I would have more difficulty looking away.

What is it with these Nulls and their raw magnetism?

"Where were you, today?" I murmur.

"Disposing of the duke's carriage."

I blink. Right.

"He's sent men out looking for you." He rushes through that explanation as if hoping it will save him. From what, I can't say. "They were in the woods today. Searching."

I ease back on my heels, sobered by that. "They're welcome

to try. But they won't find me. Not when I don't want to be found. I'm too lucky for that."

His lips press together. "You don't want to go back?"

"No. I'd do anything not to."

His gaze flickers away, and the moment of connection passes. "Well, your luck might hold when I'm not here. But with me sitting in this chair, and you doing"—he clears his throat and waves a hand—"*that*...anything could happen. They could find this place."

Ice coasts down my spine. He's right, and the prospect of discovery casts a chill into my marrow. I can't let the duke's men haul me to the altar before I've convinced Jack to banish my Mark.

He sighs. "If anyone's out there... It's just chance right now. For as long as I'm in this room, neither of us has any luck, good or bad. Which means I should go."

He's right, and I hate it. I hate that sharing space exposes us.

"But you'll come again tomorrow?" I say.

"Just for a minute."

My attention drifts past him to the windows. No lights or lanterns bob in the woods, but I feel painfully vulnerable all of the sudden. Anyone roaming out there would probably glimpse the firelight from a quarter mile off.

Jack rises from the chair and carefully maneuvers around me. When he reaches the door, I remember to ask.

"How is she? Your friend?"

He turns so the firelight catches his profile, and I startle. I can't understand why I thought of him as plain-faced yesterday, because even beneath the mask, the lines of his face hint at boldness.

"Better." True warmth seeps into his voice. Whoever the woman on the other side of the wall is, he cares about her. "A little, at least. Thank you for that."

"Could I visit her, maybe?"

He tenses. "Better not. She needs all the rest she can get right now."

"Oh," I say. "Okay. I won't bother her, then."

"Thank you." He reaches for the doorknob.

"Jack?"

"Yes? Do you need—" He turns to face me fully. And abruptly cuts off.

I try to imagine what I look like, kneeling here before the fire, backlit and glowing, with my braid hanging over one shoulder and my palms braced on my thighs.

Whatever he sees, it makes him hover there for far too long, his expression caught between a plea and a warning. Not that I can see much with that mask covering everything. But I get the gist, regardless.

"I can't go back," I tell him softly. "If I have to marry the duke, I'll die."

"Then I'll stay away," he says. "I'll make sure no one finds you."

I consider that. "There's another option, you know."

He sets his jaw. "Oh?"

"Yes." I hunt for my courage. Thankfully, it's easier to locate when I'm not face-to-face with Weston. "You could touch me again. For longer, this time."

A choked sound comes from his throat.

"Not," I hasten to add, "that I'm trying to seduce you, or anything. I just... I don't want it. My Mark. I never have. I'd rather just be normal."

He stands frozen, his gloved hand on the doorhandle. "You hate your luck that much?"

I dig my thumbs into the priceless, buttery silk of my nightgown. "I hate that it dictates everything about my life. Where I can go, who I can touch. Who I have to marry."

"Right." He laughs, short and hard and barren, as if I've just imparted deeply unpleasant news. "So you're asking a Null to touch you. Of course that's why."

I frown. He thinks I'm trying to use him, clearly. "Touching me would free you, too."

Another merciless laugh. "Yes, but what you're asking... It can't be undone. If you regretted...I'd have to live with that for the rest of my life."

"I wouldn't," I say. "Regret it."

"You don't know that. Not for sure."

I clench my fists, but I have no way to refute that. "Please."

He shakes his head, short and sharp, and hauls his gaze from mine. "It's not going to happen. I'm sorry."

Before I can answer, he slips out into the night.

This time, he doesn't even say goodbye.

Chapter Ten

A week passes.

Each morning, I rise early and listen to the woman across the wall. Day by day, her coughing eases, gradually replaced by even breaths that filter through the stone. I spend long hours curled in bed, keeping vigil with a book in hand. While my unseen charge heals, I lose myself in one fantastical world after the next.

Jack, true to his word, mostly stays away. He plunks a bag of food onto the counter each evening, then turns and walks right back out again. Each time, disappointment sits heavy in my gut. I want to invite him to stay. Entice him back to the fireside and ask him to work the tangles from my hair. I want to work the tangles from *him*.

But fear of discovery keeps my jaw locked tight. According to Jack, the duke's men venture further into the woods each day.

For as long as he remains distant, I'm protected—if the duke's lackeys stray too close, they'll inevitably suffer a

SHAYLIN GANDHI

snakebite to the ankle, or a tree will fall and bar their way. Something.

But if Jack lingers here, I become vulnerable, and dread swirls in my gut when I imagine being discovered. Being dragged away and chained to a life of lovelessness. Meaning-lessness.

Still, after a week of non-stop reading, punctuated by evening glasses of milk, an idle restlessness sets in. I've never gone this long without human interaction, and the isolation that felt so freeing a week ago now tips toward the claus-trophobic.

I can't hide here forever, alone. Something has to give.

So, when Jack arrives that night, I throw caution to the wind.

I hold out the hairbrush. He eyes it with skepticism, but ultimately sighs and traipses over to the chair by the fire, tilting it to keep himself ensconced in shadow. He sits and fiddles with his mask until it obscures even *more* of his face. "Let's be quick," he says in that gravelly baritone.

I take my place on the floor between his knees. I chose my flimsiest nightgown tonight, mostly in an effort to entice him, but he seems tragically unaffected. He makes quick, utilitarian strokes with the brush and plaits my hair with a deftness that shocks me.

He must have been holding out on me, that first time. Lingering, whether he meant to or not. Because tonight, he seems almost...harried.

"What's wrong?"

Jack's gloved hands still in my hair. "What? Nothing."

I roll my eyes, even though he can't see it. "Come on. Something's bothering you."

78

He's quiet for a moment. "Why do you say that?"

I lift a shoulder and drop it again. "It's obvious."

For long heartbeats, he just breathes. "Okay. Fine. If you really want to know, the duke's men are getting closer. It's like they know where to look. Which I realize is just my curse. They'll go wherever I do, without even realizing it. But that means I had to spend the day running in circles. Leading them away from this place. And it's tiring. I'm tired."

My insides squeeze. He has his own reasons for doing this, I know. He needs me here so the mystery woman can heal. And yet I appreciate his efforts more than I can say.

"How'd you know?" he says quietly. "That something was weighing on me?"

"Because." I hug my knees tighter. "You're not that hard to read. You're not half as mysterious as you think."

He lays the braid against my shoulder, finished now. "Mysterious? I don't think I'm mysterious at all."

I can't help but smile. "Really? Why wear all that black, then? The gloves? The long shirt? The mask?"

He grunts. "Because. I don't want to touch you by accident. And I happen to like black."

"But the mask? You do realize it's unnecessary, right? I've already seen your face. I saw it the day you kidnapped me."

He's quiet. "Maybe for a second. But I don't need you picking me out of a line-up, after this is over. With my luck, I'd hang for this."

My heart falters mid-beat. I may not have known him for long, but bile floods my throat when I picture him dangling from a rope. "I wouldn't turn you in. Not ever. Not after the favor you've done me."

"A favor." A sigh bleeds out of him. "Is that what this is?"

79

"Yes," I say emphatically.

"Was your life really so bad?"

"Well, no." My eyes lock on the flames without really seeing them. "Of course not. It's just that it wasn't my own. This stupid Mark is supposed to give me everything, but it's never actually worked out that way. Mostly, it's kept me coddled. Pinned under my family's thumb. It's wrapped me up in a nice, pretty cage."

He swallows thickly, and I get the sense he's gathering his thoughts. "I believe that. I believe *you*. But being charmed has to be better than being cursed."

I shift. He's right, which is precisely why my discontent is so hard to explain. I sound ungrateful. Spoiled.

I am those things, probably.

But I want so badly to be more. I want the chance to grow past all that.

"Not," Jack says, "that it's a contest. Because I've thought a lot about what you said. About your life being artificial. And it sounds stifling."

The concession reaches into me and lays a warm hand against my heart. "It feels that way sometimes," I say softly. "But what's life like for you? Being a Null?"

He makes a gruff sound of surprise. I wait, giving him room to consider.

It's a question I never dared to ask Weston. Because, for all that I've spent ten years pining for that man, we never existed in easy closeness like this. He always came to visit Brendan, and though he lingered to talk to me in the library, or the hallway, or anywhere, really—wherever I happened to be that day —the interlude never lasted as I wanted it to. Brendan would always tug him away. I'd stick close to them, afterward, mostly to negate Weston's Mark, but he and I didn't have many chances to speak candidly like this, alone.

Jack grunts. "It's...hard to explain. And it's probably different than you think, because I can deal with the bad things. I'm used to them now. It doesn't bother me anymore that I can't sleep through the night because my blanket's always falling off, or I'll roll over and sprain my thumb, or a mouse will decide to start chewing on my toe, or—"

"A mouse?" My hand flies to my mouth. "*Chewed* on you? That actually happened?"

A low chuckle rumbles out of him, and I startle. It's the first time I've heard him laugh.

"You sound surprised."

"I am." I twist around.

He gazes down, his eyes a faint glint in the darkness. "What, you think my curse leaves me alone at night? Because it doesn't. It doesn't leave me alone ever. And *that's* the hard part—not that bad things always happen, but that I don't know what they'll be. Which direction they'll come from. It's like my heart's always beating a million miles an hour. I'm just...on alert, all the time, waiting to see what Fortuna will come up with next. And that feeling always gets worse when I'm with people. Because then I'm dreading for them, too. Waiting for something to happen and for it to be my fault. And I hate that. I hate being a burden."

His words slip between my ribs, sharp. Aimed. Is this how Weston feels? Like he's always on the brink of something disastrous, and he's just waiting to find out what? Like his mere existence is an inconvenience for everyone else?

It must be.

At the thought, my heart tilts on its axis. I miss him like

he's been carved out of me, yet the fresh flood of longing rearing up in me feels...different tonight. Half of me wants the Null I left behind, while the other half wants to be right here. Because when I look at Jack now, my heartbeat stutters in nearly the same way it did with Weston.

Slowly, carefully, I set the brush aside. I rise up on my knees and brace my forearms on Jack's legs.

A hiss skates in through his lips. His thighs flex beneath my touch, the muscles cording with tension. The firelight paints his shirt in shades of flickering gold.

"Bria," he says, hoarse. "What're you doing?"

"It's okay," I whisper. A layer of thick black fabric insulates my skin from his. "We're not touching. And you don't have to dread, around me. You don't have to worry at all. You can just relax for a minute. Be yourself. Let go."

A pained sound escapes him. His eyes flutter closed.

I wait for what feels like an eon, just...resting against him. Existing with him. I wonder if he ever allows himself this much with anyone else. Judging by his description of his love life, I'd wager not.

Jack's gloved hand twitches at his side. When he reaches out, I expect him to push me away, but he doesn't.

His fingers take hold of mine.

I startle. Then stare at the stark contrast—black leather against pale skin. It's just his hand, and yet this marks the first time since I've come here that he's yielded to me. The first time he's softened.

He opens his eyes. Goddess, I wish he'd lean forward. Let the firelight catch them so I could find out what color they are.

"You shouldn't have to live like that," I murmur. "Like what you just described."

"I should, though." He sounds exhausted, suddenly. Defeated. "Fortuna wouldn't have Marked me unless she had a reason."

The statement nearly stops my pulse. Does he really believe that? "What? No. That's not true. At all." I know because of Weston. Because he did nothing to warrant Fortuna's disapproval.

"It is," Jack says.

"It's not." My voice rises. "You don't deserve your triquetra any more than I do mine. You can't honestly tell me you think I've done something to earn this thing."

"Of course I can."

I frown.

"All I have to do," he says, "is look at you to know you're special. That the goddess chose you for a reason. And if that's true for you...it must be true for me, too."

The sentiment settles in my chest like a stone. It's an enormous thing to say. Especially to a near-stranger. "Jack, that's..."

But I trail off, because he finally shifts. The firelight touches his eyes, and there's something about the way he's looking at me. A wall has come down, and behind it, I glimpse a sprawl of pain and resignation and longing.

One that's wholly familiar. Because I've looked into eyes like this before, peered through onto this very same tangle of repressed feeling. I've caught this exact shade of light brown studying me from across a room.

Suspicion feathers along the back of my mind. Which makes no sense, because I *saw* Jack's face, on the road that day. And yet...

I need to see it again. I need to understand who I'm talking to, how he can draw me into his gravity like this. Because only one other person has ever been able to do that.

I draw a steadying breath, disentangle our hands, and reach for him.

His spine goes rigid. "Don't."

It's a warning, but I don't relent, and he doesn't actually do anything to stop me. My fingers graze his mask, the fabric a whisper against my skin.

His lips part on a sharp inhale. I lean in and slide a finger beneath the cloth, tugging it away from his face. But I make sure not to touch him directly. I don't need to, for this.

"Bria, no." He sounds broken and terrified.

"Shh," I say. "It's okay."

"It's—"

A shout echoes outside.

I freeze. Jack's eyes pop wide. My heart lodges in my throat.

For long moments, we just stare at one another.

Then, after the most fraught silence of my life, he says, "Shit. The duke."

Chapter Eleven

An instant later, Jack is on his feet. He grips me by the arms and levers me up. "Stay here," he orders. "Don't move an inch."

Fear ices my veins. Fortuna, I shouldn't have asked him to linger. I shouldn't have risked discovery, even for a moment. Now I've endangered both of us.

But there's no accusation in Jack's eyes, only fear armored by determination. "I won't let them take you." He spins away, fists curling at his sides.

My hand flutters to the base of my throat. He intends to face them, then. To take on Alverton's men. Alone. With his cursed luck.

"Wait," I hiss, but he's already at the door. He shoots me a look over his shoulder, his eyes twin flames in the dark.

Stay put, they say.

Then he's gone, the door snicking shut behind him.

My pulse beats a staccato drum in my ears. Voices filter in from outside, sharp and excited.

I should probably do as Jack says. Stay put, where my luck

can save me. He might already be far enough away for it to work.

But...

Dread claws up my throat. If I'm alone with my luck, then so is he, and his Mark could be his undoing. He could be killed out there, trying to protect me. At the very least, he'll be captured and turned over to the law.

Before I can complete the thought, I'm moving, my feet carrying me to the door. I yank it open. Outside, the night is moonless, the only light coming from the stars scattered across the sky.

And the torches. At the treeline, two strangers hold flickering flames aloft, their features distorted by the wavering light.

Jack stands halfway across the clearing, facing them with his fists raised.

Except...Fortuna help me.

That's not Jack.

My chest seizes, my entire body draining of blood. I would recognize that stance in the dark. I *do* recognize it in the dark, because I've clocked its lethal grace a thousand times, felt my heart tugged along by the rise and fall of those fists like a puppet bound by strings.

That's Weston standing there, with his chin tucked and ready to brawl. Every line of his body looks precisely the same as it does in the ring.

For a moment, I can't speak. I can't even breathe.

The sturdier of the duke's lackeys steps forward, his wolfish gaze fixed on me. "Well, lookey here. You wouldn't happen to be that Charm that went missing last week, now, would you?"

Weston glances back at me. "I thought I told you to stay inside," he snaps, but there's no heat in it.

"I..." My throat has gone dry. That's the man I love, under that mask. The one I thought abandoned me. "I couldn't."

The invading men venture closer, and Weston turns back to them with a snarl. And goddess, the sound is so very *him* that I can't believe I didn't recognize him, even with that gravelly voice he affected.

Except maybe I did. Maybe my body knew him without conveying the message to my brain.

"Leave us alone," Weston says. "We don't like trespassers showing up in the middle of the night, and we don't know anything about any Charm."

The duke's lackey sneers. "No? Then why're you dressed like a highwayman? Big coincidence, seeing as how one stole the duke's wife last week."

I almost shout that I'm no wife of the duke's, not yet, but I hold back. Not that it matters. Weston has no excuse for his attire, nothing that will convince these men he's anything other than the criminal who kidnapped Alverton's intended.

The other man raises his torch to cast me in a brighter light. He sucks on his teeth and hocks a gob of spit. "That's gotta be her. Look. Long brown hair, just like Alverton said. Pretty, too."

At that, Weston makes a murderous sound.

"They're two of us," the smaller man warns. "And only one of you. So you might as well hand her over. Maybe if you do, you won't hang."

A silent scream explodes inside my skull. I won't let Weston die for me. I can't. I'd sooner marry the duke and be miserable for the rest of my life.

"Stop," I shout to him. "Just let them take me."

But Weston doesn't listen. He advances, a blur of black in the night. When he reaches the first man—the bigger one—he feints left, then swings right. His fist connects. A sickening crack rings out across the clearing.

The man goes pinwheeling into the grass. Weston wastes no time turning to the second, who squares his shoulders and drops into a surprisingly competent stance.

My stomach twists. After having witnessed Weston's many fights, I can tell when an opponent will pose a challenge and when he won't.

This one will. He tosses his torch aside. It sizzles in the dewy grass. A moment later, he and Weston come together, a whirl of fists and fury.

Blows connect. Pained grunts erupt, punctuated by labored breaths. They trade punch after punch, the other man with a quickness that matches his size, Weston with efficient brutality.

But brutality won't be enough, not with his curse. Not with me standing in the cabin's doorway, thirty feet away.

The moment I think it, Weston stumbles and goes down. A root, perhaps, or a rock. It doesn't matter. The man he's fighting seizes the advantage, pulling back his fist to deliver a savage punch.

"No!" The cry tears from my throat. I break into a run.

Weston's head whips toward me, his expression panicked, but I don't slow. I seek him like an aimed arrow. If I get close enough, I can grant him an even playing field, at least.

"Stay back," he shouts.

I don't.

The thin man's fist crashes into his face, and a scream

erupts from my chest. It feels like someone's ripped my heart out. Not cleanly, either. The thing is a bloody mess, arteries and tendons trailing, globules of red spattered all over the place.

I'll never get used to seeing Weston hurt.

But he absorbs the blow without any fanfare. He kicks out, tripping the other man, then struggles with whatever made him stumble—a vine, apparently, tangled around his leg. The moment I draw near enough to nullify his luck, he yanks the thing off and surges upward. He drives a shoulder into his opponent's midsection just as the man finds his feet.

I'm on the verge of cheering when sturdy arms grab me from behind.

I scream and flail, pummeling my captor with angry fists. Somehow, the bigger one got behind me. He grunts beneath the force of my blows, but doesn't relent. He just hauls me backward, away from the fray.

Panic licks along my nerves. No. No, no, no. If he drags me any further, Weston's curse will flare to life again.

I fling out an elbow, catching my assailant in what feels like the nose, because something rubbery gives way with a crunch. The man howls. The hold around my midsection eases.

Pure, dumb luck. The real kind, this time.

I dart away, or try to, but he catches the back of my night-gown, checking my forward momentum. I jerk to a stop, straining against his hold.

Weston throws a punch that lays his opponent out, then pivots toward me. When he takes in my situation, undiluted fury floods his face. "Birdie!"

My heart clenches like a fist. *Birdie*. That one word has me doubling my efforts, pitching forward in an effort to reach him. But the man behind me hauls on my gown, keeping me in place.

Weston's focus shifts past me. "If you don't let her go right this second, I promise you I will *break* something."

The man only pulls harder. I lash out with a bare foot and catch him somewhere that must hurt, because he yelps. His grip vanishes. I stumble free. Weston stomps toward me, forgetting his other opponent entirely.

Which proves to be a mistake. The smaller man leaps his feet. Something glints in his hand—a knife, it looks like, catching the torchlight. He lunges after Weston.

My blood surges hot in my veins. Once again, I react without thinking. I dart past Weston and throw myself at the knife-wielder just as he slashes.

I hit him in the elbow, altering the blade's trajectory. It catches Weston's shirt, opening a nick in the fabric without breaking skin.

We go crashing to the ground. Pain erupts all along my side. The blade skitters into the dirt.

Weston doesn't seem to register the close call. Stark fury has swallowed him up, narrowing his focus, and now he won't stop until he destroys something. He stomps to where the larger man lies on the ground, grabs hold of his arm, and twists. A sharp crack ricochets through the clearing.

The man screams.

I stare from my place in the grass, my jaw slack. Eight. That's eight bones Weston has broken now in my defense.

When I manage to catch the breath my fall knocked out of me, I haul myself upright. But the smaller man catches my hair and yanks, wrenching my head back. Pain ignites in my scalp. A line of chilly fire is pressed to my throat.

It's...the knife. Digging into my neck. I go still.

Weston whirls to face us. And freezes.

Silence pummels my ears. How'd the smaller one retrieve the knife so quickly? And how'd he grab me so fast?

Bad luck, I guess. Nothing more.

My captor pulls my hair so hard my spine arches. Tears gather in my eyes. The knife pricks the skin beneath my jaw.

"Alverton said we could bring her back a little scratched up," my captor says, "if necessary. Which means if you don't stay over there, he's going to get her back half-dead."

Cold rage overtakes Weston's face. His mask has been torn away in the scuffle, and in the light of the fallen torches, he looks both terrifying and hewn from gold—gold hair, golden eyes, golden skin stretched over hard features. When our gazes lock, that single moment of eye contact drives the breath from me all over again.

He's so unapologetically, cruelly beautiful. I can see it even with a knife pressed to my throat.

"If you spill a drop of her blood," he says, dark and deadly, "you won't leave this clearing alive. I swear it."

The man gripping me hesitates, I can *feel* it. "I didn't realize we'd be up against a pugilist," he mutters.

"Well, guess what." Weston's fists flex at his sides. "You are. And that *pugilist* has no qualms about adding *murderer* to his calling card."

For long moments, no one moves, except for the injured man. He struggles to his knees, his face ashen, his broken arm cradled gingerly in front of him. A dribble of red leaks from one nostril.

Weston doesn't pay him an ounce of attention. His eyes flicker between my face and the blade at my throat. A fleeting arrow of fear races across his features, then disappears behind a steely wall.

He takes a step backward. Then another.

Panic jolts through me. What is he doing? He's not...abandoning me, is he? But then I realize. My luck. He's giving it room to work.

"Wait," the man holding me says. "What're you—"

Weston must cross out of range, because a streak of white and brown swoops from the darkness. My captor shrieks. Wings and talons flash. The knife vanishes from its place at my throat as the man scuffles with what looks like...an owl?

Fortuna's blessings, I don't waste time figuring it out. I just hurtle toward Weston, who meets me halfway and catches me by the shoulders, holding me at arm's length to stop me from burrowing against him.

A pang stabs through me. Even now. Even here.

"Get behind me," he says.

"I'm not going to—"

"Birdie," he growls, a naked command. "Get. Behind. me. Now."

I squeak and station myself behind him, sticking close enough to neutralize his luck. I won't abandon him, no matter what he says.

The smaller man finally bats the attacking owl away. The bird sails off into the night, leaving a handful of bloody scratches behind.

The man's lip curls. He scrubs at his ruined cheek and fixes on me. "Witch," he says. "Demon."

I blink. *Witch*. Huh. That's one I haven't gotten before.

Weston raises his fists again, but otherwise, no one moves, the fight apparently at an impasse.

I take a quick inventory. The other man has a knife. We have Weston's skill. And no luck to speak of, good or bad.

Which probably renders our chances an even fifty-fifty.

My mind spins, searching for ways to tip the balance. If that man gets near us with his blade, this could go catastrophically wrong, and I can't allow that to happen. But we can't let him leave, either. He'll only return with rein-forcements.

Then I land on an idea that sticks. One I can make work. I think.

I hope.

"You work for the duke?" I call over Weston's shoulder.

The armed man narrows his eyes. He holds his knife loosely and with a disturbing degree of familiarity. "Wouldn't be here, if we didn't."

I ignore the patent condescension in his tone. "Alverton's paying you, then? How much?"

"Birdie?" Weston whispers from the side of his mouth. "What're you doing?"

"Bribing them," I whisper back.

The duke's man scans me with hateful eyes. "Enough to make this worth it."

"Nothing's worth this," the larger one interjects, hunched over his ruined arm.

I seize on that. "No, nothing is worth this, is it? Risking injury? Death? You'd be better off letting me top the duke's price, because I can give you enough to last you months. You wouldn't have to work for Alverton anymore. You wouldn't have to work at all."

The smaller man's expression twitches, hardening into something I recognize, because I've seen that look on Brendan's face plenty of times. Calculation. *Hunger.*

"How much are we talking?" he ventures.

"I have a hairbrush," I say. "Inside. Sterling silver and gold. It's worth a small fortune, just by itself."

Skepticism passes over his face.

"And a brooch," I hasten to add. "Rubies and diamonds. *Lots* of diamonds."

He makes a thoughtful sound. "Hmm."

"You can have them. All you have to do is leave us alone. And make sure the duke doesn't find out we're here."

Weston grumbles a protest, but I silence him with a tug on his shirt. I know he'd rather make these men pay the same way Theodore did—with pain and blood and suffering—but I can't let him risk himself.

The lackeys exchange looks, weighing their options. They don't have many. They can either fight and risk Weston's wrath, or take my offer.

The smaller man spits on the ground. "Fine."

My heartbeat catches. "You'll do it?"

"For that price, I'd be stupid not to."

"And you won't tell anyone where we are? Or come back?"

His jaw works. "No. I swear it. But you'd better pay up."

My attention slides to the man with the broken arm. "And you?"

He regards Weston for long moments, his eyes burning with resentment. I hold my breath.

"Yes," he finally says. "Deal."

I nearly sag. But I shore myself up with fistfuls of Weston's shirt and tug him backward toward the cabin with me. No way am I leaving him alone out here, at the mercy of his bad luck.

Inside, I dig through my trunk for the brooch. It's one my mother bought on a whim, utterly meaningless and without sentimental value. I palm the thing and retrieve the hairbrush I abandoned near the hearth.

Weston crosses his arms and scowls. "You're sure about this?"

I give him a look. One he knows me well enough to interpret. "Of course. These're just things. Useless ones."

He peers down at the objects in my hands. "Maybe, but I've never owned anything that valuable. I can't imagine having them, much less giving them away."

"Losing them's better than letting those men report back to the duke. And it's definitely better than you trying to kill them and ending up hurt."

He snorts. "I'd gladly kill them, for you. And I'd succeed. I'd *enjoy* it."

That brings me up short, but I swallow past the sudden thickness in my throat. If he thinks he can distract me from the very incendiary conversation we're about to have—about him *lying* to me for over a week—he's sorely mistaken.

"Weston," I say.

His jaw flexes. "Birdie."

"Get out of my way."

"No. Give me those. I'm not letting you anywhere near those two."

I contemplate, then do as he asks.

Outside, the duke's men watch with wary eyes as Weston approaches. I stick close to him, shielded by the breadth of his body.

When we draw near, I see that sweat has broken out on the injured man's brow. The smaller one's eyes jump back and forth like he's trying to puzzle out the dynamic between Weston and me.

"Sorceress," he mutters. "Temptress."

Weston stiffens, but I yank on his sleeve to keep him from surging forward. Which probably only strengthens the impression that I've somehow ensorcelled my kidnapper.

I only wish that were true. Goddess help me, how I wish that were true.

"Take these." Weston practically throws the brooch and brush. "And don't come back. And if you tell the duke about us, I'll hunt you. And find you. And do very, very bad things to you, once I do."

The bigger man blanches. The second scans Weston with hard eyes, then gives a grudging nod.

When they stagger away into the trees, Weston turns to me.

The cabin glows behind me, its thrown light gilding the austere lines of his face. He doesn't even have the grace to look contrite. "So," he says. "I guess we need to talk about this."

"Yeah." I snort. "I'd say so."

Chapter Twelve

Inside of ten seconds, it turns into a fight.

Of course it does.

I stand by the fireplace, trying to soothe the scorch of my anger with the gentle warmth of the flames. But my skin feels too tight, my blood whirring with equal parts rage and relief.

Goddess, Weston could have been killed out there. Weston, not Jack, because *he's* the one who stole me. Jack doesn't actually exist. Whoever I saw on the road that day was...a decoy, probably. Just another layer of the lie. Because after I saw that man's face, I lost sight of him, at least for a minute or two.

A minute or two in which Weston must have taken over.

"How dare you?" I whirl and fling an accusing finger at him. "What in the world made you think it was okay to trick me like that? To lie?"

He stands just out of reach, his arms crossed, his eyes guarded. "I didn't lie." He's abandoned that growling voice, at least, and now sounds like himself again.

"Yes, you did," I hiss. "You told me your name was Jack. You told me you *lived* here. You said there was some woman on the other side of a wall you needed me to save."

"My name *is* Jack." His lip curls, the makings of a snarl. As if all it takes to spark his anger is to feel the flare of mine. "It's my middle name. Weston Jackson Wildes."

I narrow my eyes. He's never told me that before.

"And I do live here," he continues.

"No, you live in town." I hurl the words, at least ninety percent sure they're true. I've heard Brendan talk about Weston's place in Pine's End, though I don't know where it is, exactly.

"I rent a room there, that's it." He leans in, which somehow grants him another inch of height. If he's going for imposing, he's definitely succeeding. "But it's a hovel. I only sleep there when I'm doing the books for the mill. They won't let me on the property while the machinery's running, and I like to be alone, anyway. But whenever I'm not working, I come here. I get *away*."

"Away? From?"

"Everything!" He glares from beneath flattened brows. "The stares. The whispers. The fact that horrible things happen to anyone who comes near me. I built this place so I'd have somewhere that was mine. Even though it took me years. Even though everything kept going wrong."

At that, I wilt a little, losing steam. The sentiment threads a hot wire through my heart and pulls it clean out the other side.

"And there is a woman across the wall," he continues darkly.

"Who?" I do my utmost to rally. If I don't keep hold of my

anger, I'll only embarrass myself. I'll probably burst into tears and beg him to touch me again, like I did at the mill. "Who is it I've been helping all this time? Your girlfriend? Or one of those lovers you're so quick to get away from? Were you just using me to fix her so you could send me back to the duke?"

"Fortuna's curses." He slams his eyes closed and pinches between them with gloved fingers. "You don't get it, Birdie. You really, truly, absolutely and completely *do not fucking get it*, do you?"

"No, I don't. Of course I don't! How could I, when I have no clue what this was for?" Fresh ire bristles hot in my chest, all my frustration of the last few weeks boiling over. "You walked away from me, Weston. You let Brendan sell me to that awful man and just...just *left*. Then you apparently changed your mind and stole me, only you told me you were someone else, and then you gave me all these books and made me cure your girlfriend, which, to be fair, I would've done anyway, if you'd just asked, and then you got me all that milk, and you... You..."

I run out of air. My lungs heave, trying to suck down more, only he's standing closer than he was a moment ago. Much closer. He bends his head, staring down into my face, and it hits me. Finally.

"You kissed me," I finish. The words slide from my tongue, molten.

Because Fortuna help me. Eight days ago, in the duke's carriage, I kissed Weston. *Weston Wildes.* The man I've hungered after for a decade. And he kissed me back. With fire and fervor and everything I've dreamed he might hold locked up in his heart.

My hand rises, unbidden, to my mouth. Weston's eyes track the movement with unerring focus.

"And you have no idea why I did all that?" he says, still watching my fingers. The question comes out smooth and oiled, like a threat. "None at all?"

"I...don't."

"You can't even *begin* to guess? You don't find it painfully obvious by now?"

"Because I asked you to?" I say, breathy. "Because I begged you to steal me?"

"Yes, because you asked." His tone rises. "And because I couldn't stand to see you as terrified as you were in your foyer. Because Brendan won't let me marry you, but I can't seem to let you marry anyone else. Because I'd rather keep you here like some museum treasure no one can touch than let the duke lay a finger on you. Because I wanted you to have books and milk and a comfortable place to sleep without you owing anyone anything, and I wanted you to be mine to watch over. For just a few days, I wanted you to be mine. So yes, I stole you. And misled you. And you can hate me for that, if you like. I probably made sure of it the moment I jumped onto the duke's carriage."

I gape at him. "I..." My voice has fled somewhere. Gotten lodged between the floorboards, out of my reach.

Weston's nostrils flare. He's so close now I can smell him, clean and salted and male, with an underlying hint of amber. He doesn't usually venture this far into my personal space, so I've never gotten a proper nose full of him before. Except maybe while we had our tongues in each other's mouths, but I was too lost in delirium then to take it in.

"And the person you're saving isn't my *girlfriend*." His eyes spark, his jaw working like he's trying to chew something in half. "I don't have a girlfriend. I don't ever have a girlfriend. The woman in that bed is my aunt."

Aunt. The word drops through me. I didn't realize Weston has relatives. At least not that he's in touch with. Because his mother...

"I thought you didn't talk to them anymore," I say. "Your family."

His lip curls. "I don't. My mom stays away. She knows better than to get anywhere near me. But my aunt... Well. She's always written me letters. Even though I've never answered. I don't know what made her decide to come looking for me after all these years, but look what it almost cost her. At least now she's learned her lesson. Finally. The way everyone—"

He bites down, cutting himself off, but I know what he was going to say.

Everyone always does.

All at once, the high peaks of my anger give way, unable to withstand the reminder of how much he hates himself.

Or the realization that Weston did all this for me. I think. And for his aunt. And for himself, maybe, in some convoluted way that tucks a seed of hope into my palm and closes my fingers around it.

"Why pretend to be someone else, though?" I say, quieter now. "Why make sure I saw that man on the roadside, before you stole my carriage?"

He looks away. "So the duke wouldn't know where to look. So even you would think I was a stranger."

"But why? Who was that man?"

"Just someone with hair like mine. Someone I hired to be seen."

I make a thick sound in the back of my throat. "But why trick *me*? The duke...fine, but me? Was it so I wouldn't turn you in, like you said? So you wouldn't have to answer to the law?"

"No." An angry line wrinkles the bridge of his nose. "I don't care if you tell the police. Go ahead. If they end up hanging me for this, it'll probably be no more than I deserve."

All the blood dives out of my cheeks. "No. What? I wouldn't. I couldn't. I can't stand the thought of a world without you in it."

He laughs, sharp and quick and cold. "You're going to have to, Birdie. We both know I'm on borrowed time. If it's not the hangman's noose, it'll be something else. I'll probably walk under a window just as someone tosses out something heavy. Or I'll step on a nail and get tetanus. I'll eat the wrong sort of mushroom while everyone else at the table lucks out with the edible kind."

I can't help myself. I grab his forearm and squeeze. Hard.

He doesn't flinch, like he would have a few weeks ago. He doesn't even move. His arm is like corded steel in my grip, his skin hot through the fabric. He watches me so intently that I feel the force of it in my toes.

"That's so..." I swallow the fresh horror pooling in my throat. "...easily avoidable."

"No," he says. "It's not."

The fire cracks and snaps, begging for attention, but we both ignore it. In the pause, Weston's gaze slides downward.

For the first time in my life, he traces a path from my eyes to my chin, then downward further still.

He settles on my Mark, which peeps through the neckline of my nightgown. "You want to know why I couldn't let you know? It had nothing to do with the law. It was so you wouldn't ask me to touch you again. So I wouldn't be tempted. Because *that*"—he rests a gloved finger against my chest—"is what saved you tonight. That man had a knife to your throat, and I couldn't help you, Birdie. I couldn't *do anything*. Not without putting you at risk. But that Mark could. So call it stifling if you want. Hate it if you want, but this is your insurance. And mine. It's the thing that lets me know you're protected, anywhere you go, all the time. And if I have to buy that guarantee with an early end, so be it."

I cease to breathe. So many things are happening inside me at once, Weston's words crashing over me in waves. All he seems to care about is keeping me safe. The revelation kindles a fragile dream in my heart, even as his bleak outlook breaks it.

He lifts his eyes from my Mark. Anguish flickers there, quickly shuttered away.

"Why do you..." The words tangle on my tongue, so I try again. "Why do you care so much?"

The firelight plays across the hard planes of his face. His hand falls from my triquetra. "You don't want to hear it. Trust me."

I press a splayed palm to my chest, as if I can trap the memory of his touch against my skin. The space beneath feels hollow, just waiting to be filled up. "I do, though. I want to hear it more than anything."

"Why?" An edge of despair slices through the word. "Why

bother? I mean, I'll admit, I thought...that there was something in the way you looked at me, maybe. You'd do it for too long, sometimes. Too often. But I get it now."

"Do you?"

"Yes." His mouth twists. He yanks at his collar, wrenching his shirt open to bare his triquetra. "You see this and it looks like an opportunity to you. It looks like a way out. *That* was why you asked me to touch you at the mill."

The absurdity of that makes me sway on my feet. That's not it. At all. I mean, his Mark *does* look like a way out, but that's entirely beside the point. I crave Weston because he's Weston. Because when I stand in front of him, I'm safe. Because here, under the force of his glare, is where I feel most at home.

"That's ridiculous," I say.

Resignation etches grooves beside his mouth. "It's not."

"It is. And I want you to say it. Whatever you're not telling me." *Please*, I silently amend. *Please let us be talking about what I think we are.*

He scowls. "There's no point."

My nails bite into my palms. Joy and frustration war within me, the clash threatening to tear me apart. "Yes. There is. Say it."

"Why?" He steps back. "So you can smile at me the way everyone else does? Like you pity me? So I'll know for sure that the thing I fooled myself into believing was never real?"

My breath speeds, a chaotic whirl in my lungs. "No. So I can say it back."

He freezes, and for once, the anger drains from his features. They're no less harsh for it, no less unforgiving, but they're softened in some faint way by surprise. Haloed with disbelief.

Something inside me cries his name. I can't believe he doesn't realize. I can't believe he believes a single word of the nonsense he just spouted.

Only...I understand why. Life, in all its relentless cruelty, has divested him of his ability to hope.

But maybe I can give him a reason. If he can give me one, too.

"Just say it," I plead.

His throat works. He blinks a few times, hard and fast. "Fine. If you're so desperate to know, then here it is: I've been cursed twice in my life. Once when I was born. And again when I met you."

A vast ache opens inside me. Something is coming, so hard and fast I'll never be the same. I'm standing in front of the avalanche as it comes careening down the mountain. In another moment, it will engulf me.

"Because..." Weston swallows hard. "You have to know, Birdie. There's no way you don't realize I've been horribly, wretchedly, agonizingly in love with you since the day we met. Ever since I was fifteen."

I close my eyes. I wanted to believe it, and yet I couldn't, not really. Not until this moment. Now radiance pours into me, a physical force, like rivers of light spilling through my veins. I become a star, burning away the dark. I'm incandescent.

When I look again, he's halfway across the room. Halfway out the door.

"Weston." It's all I can manage. A broken whisper. An answered prayer.

He pauses mid-flight.

"I was fourteen," I say.

His shoulders tense. "I know how old you were when we met."

"No, I don't mean when we met. I mean when I fell in love. I was fourteen when I fell in love."

The tense set of his posture loosens. He pivots more slowly than I knew a man could.

"With you," I add. Just to be sure. "And I've loved you ever since. Every moment." Even when I didn't want to.

His whole body slackens, his lips parting. "What?"

"You." My voice stabilizes. "Are all I've ever wanted."

He blinks, long and hard. "You...want my Mark, you mean. You want me to touch you. To *take* from you. You want to be rid of your luck."

"No." I grab fistfuls of my nightgown to keep from running to him. My palms burn for him, to touch him, but I can't. Not if I want him to understand. "I mean, yes, of course I want you to touch me. But the important part is that I don't want you to stop, once you do. Not ever."

He stares, his breaths piling atop one another, a mess of sharp intakes and shaky exhales. I swear I see each of my words land. He blinks twice, then hauls a hand through his hair, leaving it disheveled. "That's..."

"The truth," I say. "No one's ever treated me like you have. Like a normal person. Like I'm a real live woman with thoughts and feelings. No one's ever *respected* me like you do."

He doesn't blink. Or move.

"You must realize I'm horribly, wretchedly, agonizingly in love with you, too. And it's not because of your Mark. It's because of the books you've brought me. And the milk. And the bones you've broken. And—"

All at once, he's crossing the room with long strides. When he reaches me, he takes my face in gloved hands and hauls it up to within a hairsbreadth of his. He stares into my eyes, his mouth an inch from mine.

A joyful whimper flies from my lips. Everything inside me crystallizes. I raise up on tiptoes, and it's as easy as falling. It's so effortless to finally, *finally* cross this hated distance.

But Weston pulls back from my advance, just a bit. He hovers for a moment that borders on endless, then makes a sound—purely male, infinitely frustrated—and tears himself away.

My knees nearly buckle. "No. No, what? What're you doing?"

He stalks toward the wall beside the fireplace, where he drops his head and presses curled fists against the stone, his back tight. I think he's shaking.

"Come back here and kiss me," I almost wail.

"I can't, Birdie. Curses, you *know* that."

Silence swamps me, binding my tongue.

"For all the reasons I just told you, I can't. I won't." He unleashes a bitter chuckle and pummels the wall with a fist.

I wince at the tender sound of leather against rock, but if it pains him, he gives no sign.

"All I can ever be to you is a liability. And I'm not going to take away your safety—your *future*—just so I can have one, too."

Part of me goes dark. Just dies away between one moment and the next, the light from earlier extinguished like a shuttered lantern. "No. What? What about what I want? What if I want to *give* you my future? What if I want to share it with you?"

Another chuckle, this one edged in ruthlessness. "Then I guess you'll finally find out what it's like to not get what you want."

I recoil. It's a cruel thing to say, and I know why he's doing it. To reinforce this separation. To buttress this uncrossable inch that somehow stretches across miles.

But that doesn't make it okay.

"Don't be mean," I say to his back.

He raises his head, as if girded by my accusation. "I am mean, though. You say you love me, and Fortuna help me, I love you so much, and want you so badly, that I can't see anything else, sometimes. But I. Am. Mean." He gives the wall another punch and pushes off to face me.

I press my lips together, trying to fence in the hurt that's piling in my throat.

"And I'm rude," he says. "And aggressive. And violent. I'm everything your parents warn you about, and I'm not good for you, Birdie. I can't be. No matter how much I wish I could. So don't ask me to kiss you. You should be kissing someone else. Anyone but me."

I stomp my bare foot against the floorboards, a weak protest that doesn't require the heroism of words.

"I'm going to stay away from you," he mutters, as if trying to convince the both of us. "My aunt's almost better now, anyway. I can't risk her again by being here. I never should've gotten near her in the first place. But once she leaves, you can stay. You can hide here for as long as you like. I'll do...anything. I'll lead the duke's men in circles for the rest of my life.

I'll kill anyone who gets close. Whatever you want. But I can't be here. I can't be near you."

With that, he turns and makes for the door, and this time, I don't stop him.

Because I'm wrecked. Held together by nothing but the tendrils of my rapidly fraying pride.

Fortuna help me, I'm sick to death of him walking away from me like this.

This, I vow, will be the last time I ever let him.

Chapter Thirteen

Another week crawls by.

I spend most of it in bed, listless. Knowing Weston loves me should nourish me—it's everything I've craved, laid bare and defenseless at last. Yet every time I relive those moments of confession, the memory dissolves into sticky, gluey pieces that burn my eyes and make my temples ache.

We may love each other, but we're no closer to having a future together. In fact, one has never felt further from reach.

On the sixth day of wallowing, I decide it's time to distract myself.

Instead of lounging around in my nightgown, I put on an actual dress, and the next day, I graduate to walking outside in the woods. Over the next week, the strolls become habit. I ramble beneath the cool dome of the forest, soaking up the late September sunshine, a basket hooked over my elbow. I forage for blackberries and elderberries, trusting my luck to keep me from choosing anything poisonous, and tuck inter-esting-looking pinecones and rocks in among my stash. Back at the cabin, I set out the berries for Weston as an offering. And he takes them. At least he does that.

I don't see him. Not once. He delivers my food whenever I'm out, which must mean he's close by, watching. Waiting for an opportunity to avoid me.

The knowledge makes my whole body cook to a simmer. Whether it's anger or a perverse thrill at this reverse voyeurism, I can't say.

Maybe both.

Weston's aunt continues to improve. I know because she doesn't cough anymore, and one day, I catch the tread of footsteps across the floorboards. She's up, finally. Moving around.

I cock an ear, then set aside my book and consider. Weston told me not to visit her, but...

That was before. When I hadn't yet nestled my heart in his hands. When he hadn't yet squeezed so forcefully that the pulp bulged out between his fingers.

I splay my book face-down on the table and push back my chair, my decision made. At the tiny mirror over the pump-handled sink, I finger-comb my tangled hair as best I can. A wad of brown strands comes loose in the process, and I unwind it from my fingers, wishing for a brush. But since that's not happening—my luck can't create things from thin air, only create opportunities from what already exists—I braid my hair to the best of my ability and pinch my cheeks to infuse them with color.

Then I lean toward the glass. I look... Bright, actually. Alive. Like my time outdoors has instilled me with a vitality I never enjoyed while languishing in that stuffy mansion near Pine's End.

Too bad this hale exterior conceals a heart that's withered to ash.

I force a smile, hold it until it looks convincing, then sweep out the door.

At the other side of the cabin, I hesitate after knocking. What if Weston's aunt doesn't like me? Worse, what if she *does*? What if she sees a Charm and wants me to perform some minor miracle for her? What if she wants to simper and stare, like my mother's aristocratic friends?

Or maybe she'll be like *him*. Maybe she'll be entirely sane and want me to sacrifice my luck to save her nephew.

A sour chuckle coils in my throat. Fortuna, what I wouldn't give to do exactly that.

If only he would let me.

Soft footfalls approach, making my nerves tangle. When the door swings open, I find myself face-to-face with a woman who looks remarkably like Weston—the same golden hair, the same angular features, the same piercing, tawny gaze. She's older, but age has honed her beauty to a fine edge.

I can see now why he asked me not to visit. I would've known. Right away.

"Oh," she says. Her voice is low and melodic. "It's you. The Charm."

"Hi. Yes. I'm Bria. I hope it's okay that I came over here to introduce myself." I wonder if I should extend a hand, then end up standing there, probably looking like I abandoned my manners on the roadside right around the same time Weston kidnapped me.

"Of course it is. You saved my life." Her keen eyes meet mine, and there's something in hers I like. A straightforwardness, maybe. A clarity that, while every bit as forceful as Weston's, lacks the sting his does.

She doesn't *look* like she houses a lit furnace inside her, one so overburdened and yet simultaneously neglected that it verges on exploding.

"How're you feeling?" I say.

"Better. Much, actually."

A tentative smile curves my lips. This isn't so bad. "I'm glad to hear it."

She nods. "Thank you. For sticking close. For sharing your luck with me."

I pause. It's something people almost never say to me, I realize. *Thank you.* Such a simple sentiment, and yet I can't remember Brendan or my parents ever voicing it, even once.

Then again, they probably shouldn't have to. It's not like I've gone to any effort to help them. I don't have the ability to turn my luck on and off. It just...is.

A smile crinkles the corners of the woman's eyes. "I'm Helena. Would you like to come in?"

I ponder, but I don't care anymore whether Weston would like it. "Sure."

She props the door open, and I squeeze past. Her side of the cabin proves to be a mirrored twin of mine, right down to the kitchenette and hand-crafted table by the window. Even a replica of my bookcase is in residence, though the literary selection differs significantly on this side. I spy texts on woodworking and joinery, and another on fireplace mechanics. One on digging wells.

This is Weston's half, then, and the realization makes me frown. Why build a home with two unconnected rooms, clearly intended to house two entirely separate people? Does he have more family I'm not aware of?

"Why don't I put on some tea?" Helena bustles to the fireplace, where she strikes a match. A blaze roars to life in record time. She blinks at the catching flames as if puzzled.

I neglect to point out that it's because of me. That fire-making proves nearly foolproof when I'm standing this close.

She hangs a kettle over the flames, and I glance around, wondering what I'm actually doing here. I must be lonelier than I realized. Starved for human contact.

With the kettle set, Helena motions me toward the table. We take seats across from one another, and she leans in, studying me.

Like Weston, she ignores my Mark. Her eyes never stray below my chin.

"So," she says. "Has he come to his senses yet?"

I startle. "Who? Weston?"

She gives me a look. A *come-on, let's-not-play-games-now* glance. "Yes, Weston. Has he decided to take you up on your offer?"

I open my mouth. Close it again. I guess we're skipping the small talk. "He...told you about that?"

"Oh, child." Her look turns knowing. "He didn't have to. The walls don't exactly keep secrets around here."

I flush, deep and burning. Goddess, this woman heard me confessing the innermost contents of my heart. She heard me *beg*. How humiliating.

A wry twist lifts Helena's mouth as she scans the evidence of my embarrassment. "If it's any consolation, I'd already figured you two out. Every time he came to check on me, he'd stare at that wall so long and so hard I swore he was trying to see through to the other side."

My cheeks burn hotter. "He did?"

"He did."

"Oh. Well. It's...complicated. Between us."

Her attention falls to my collarbones, but only briefly. "Yes. I can see that."

We study one another in silence. This close, the evidence of her convalescence shows—bruised shadows cling beneath her eyes and her green muslin dress hangs from a frame that was undoubtedly stouter a couple months ago. But she'll be fine, eventually. I can tell that much at a glance.

"You probably already realize this," she says, "but that boy doesn't surrender anything that isn't dragged out of him by force."

I look down, to where my hands twist in my lap. I do know that.

"So you might have to do some dragging," she adds.

I sigh. She makes it sound so straightforward, but I have no idea how to get Weston to stop fighting me. To quit pushing me away for what he thinks is my own good.

"He's convinced his curse makes him unworthy of happiness," Helena says.

I meet her gaze again. "It doesn't, though. He doesn't deserve to be punished. It's not his fault Fortuna Marked him."

"Oh, you're preaching to the choir on that one, trust me." Her smile is thin. "But try telling him that. He'd rather suffer than risk tainting anyone with his misfortune. And he's spent so long believing the world has no place for him that he can't see anything else. Even when it's staring him in the face, bold as brass."

The phrase tickles at my mind. *Bold as brass.* It's what I would have to be, probably, to break through Weston's walls. The only problem being that I'm not bold at all. Not brazen in the slightest. Fortuna hasn't exactly given me the opportunity to cultivate that side of myself.

Helena reaches across the table and pats my hand. "Just don't give up on him, is what I'm saying. He's already spent too much time giving up on himself."

The sentiment makes my chest hurt. I *won't* give up. Not because I'm some bastion of fortitude, but because I can't. Loving Weston is woven into my marrow, as vital and inescapable as breathing. The one time I tried to deny it, I got precisely nowhere.

"Not," Helena adds, her tone swerving into dark, brambly territory, "that it's his fault, really. You have to understand how hard life's been for him. My sister wasn't the best parent. She was... Is..." She sets her jaw as if doubting her next words.

"I know," I say, hoping to relieve her of the need to continue. "Weston told me."

Her head tilts. "Did he?"

I shift in my chair. "About how his mom refused to touch him when he was a kid? That she made him sleep in the kitchen so he wouldn't be anywhere near her or his siblings? That every time something went wrong, she punished him, even though his curse was never his choice? Even though sometimes, he hadn't been nearby, and whatever had happened had come down to actual luck? Yeah. He did." I end with a click of my teeth, my jaw tight.

Helena scans me with new eyes. "Well. Yes, that's it exactly.

She wouldn't even hold him when he was born. I don't think she ever did, to tell you the truth. Not once."

Outrage scalds my airway, and for a moment, I can't speak. "I hate her," I finally say. "I know I shouldn't say that, because she's your sister and everything, but whoever she is, *wherever* she is, I hate her guts."

Helena leans back. Appreciation glimmers in her eyes. After a pause, she says, "I like you. A lot."

A smile tugs at my mouth, equal part bitter and touched. "You're not so bad yourself."

She flashes a grin and goes to the kettle, returning a minute later with two teacups on saucers. She drops in the bags and offers me a cube of sugar. "No milk, I'm afraid. Weston was insistent on it all going to your side."

My chest constricts, but I sip the tea until the tightness passes. Helena and I chat for a while, mostly about inconsequential topics that feel far safer than our opening one.

When I finally drain my teacup, I carry it to the sink and work the pump handle to bring up water. I wash out my dishes, then move on to Helena's, since she's still in recovery.

Also, I just plain like her.

"Will you come see me again tomorrow?" she asks, at the door.

I smile. "I'd like that." And I mean it. Despite the fact that she reminds me of Weston, she provides a welcome distraction from the emotional debris the other night left me buried beneath.

"I'd like it, too." She smiles. "And Bria, you should know that I'm leaving. In a few days. I've had my visit—eventful as it was—and now it's time to go home."

She must catch my crestfallen expression, because she

adds, "Don't worry, it'll be better once I'm gone. It'll give you two a chance to talk. Alone."

"It won't, though." I hate how glum I sound. "Weston won't come anywhere near me."

"He will, eventually. Without me here, he'll get lonely."

My gaze sharpens. "Wait, what? Does that mean he visits you?"

At that, she looks sheepish. "Sometimes. Only for a few minutes. But...I always get the sense it's not really me he wants to see. That he's teetering on the edge, and all he needs is a push."

I huff, wanting so badly to believe that, but something hollow and hungry nips at me.

"Or maybe a good, hard shove," she tacks on.

A good, hard shove. Right.

Not exactly my area of expertise.

Back on my side of the cabin, I freeze the instant I close the door. Someone has been here. The book I left splayed face-down now lies closed on the table, a sprig of goldenrod serving as a bookmark. The sturdy canvas bag Weston uses for groceries sits on the counter, filled with bread and cheese and potatoes, while a bottle of milk sweats gently on the counter. And...

My stomach flips. There's a hairbrush. Placed carefully in front of the grocery bag, where I can't miss it.

I draw near, my pulse accelerating to a hum. I turn the brush over. It's made of wood, carved smooth and fitted with boar bristles. My initials have been seared into the back. BIR. Bria Iris Radcliffe.

A flurry of emotions pops off within me, like the

gunpowder firecrackers Brendan and I used to play with at New Year's as kids.

Weston made me this brush. For me. With his own hands.

I like it infinitely better than the last one. And I'm flabbergasted that he knew my middle name, considering I didn't know his.

Ignoring the groceries—I'll put them away later—I wander over to the dead fire and sink into the armchair. I unravel my makeshift braid and work the knots from my locks, brushing until my hair is smooth and lustrous.

Then I look down at the gift Weston made me.

"Just give him a good, hard shove," I tell it. "Bold as brass."

The words echo in the empty room.

Chapter Fourteen

Over the next few days, Helena and I take to spending long hours together, chatting amicably about nothing and everything.

It's a novel experience, because, for most of my life, female friendship has escaped me. Not out of choice. More because the one close friend I had in childhood, Holly Hendricks, turned out to not be my friend at all. When I was twelve, I overheard her confessing to our classmates that she didn't care for me all that much. She just loved how lucky she became when we were together.

I was fortunate, of course, to have found out. But the experience altered something in me. Like a broken bone that never set quite right, my faith in friendship was bent askew that day. Which was probably why I delved so enthusiastically into books, afterward.

Helena is no Holly, though. She doesn't *want* anything from me. I can't pinpoint which quality of hers makes me so certain—maybe it's her no-nonsense attitude, or her quiet aura of self-assuredness. Maybe it's both of those things.

Either way, when I'm with her, I sometimes forget I'm a Charm.

It's remarkably freeing.

I ask Helena every question I can think of. I learn that she has no children and lives in Hearthsgill, a three-day carriage journey from Pine's End. It's the same place Weston is from. The same place his whole family still lives.

The place he left when he was fifteen.

Helena asks me about my family, too, which prompts me to wonder, probably much too late, what my brother must think of my disappearance.

Does Brendan know I'm okay? That Weston is with me? Or...not with me, really, but lurking around the fringes of my life, more savior than jailer?

He must, because Weston and I vanished at the same time.

There aren't many potential explanations for that, except the truth, and the realization grips me in cold claws. But Brendan must not know about this place. If he did, he'd have shown up already, demanding I do my duty and marry Alverton.

My gut sours. I can't imagine how this all will end. At some point, I'll have to return to Pine's End, but when I do, I'll need to ensure Brendan doesn't blame his best friend for this.

Weston has taken such enormous risks for my sake. Even if he won't talk to me.

On the day Helena departs, she wraps me in a hug. She looks hale and healthy, now. The shadows beneath her eyes have faded, and no rasp taints her breathing, even when she gathers a lungful of autumn air.

She holds me close and murmurs in my ear. "Don't let him shut you out, okay?"

I cling to her, wishing she would stay. "I don't exactly have a choice."

"You always have a choice." She pulls back and taps my Mark with a bare forefinger. I nearly lose my breath at how casually she does it. Given that she shares blood with Weston, such a cavalier touch seems almost illicit, somehow. "This thing only dictates your life if you let it."

I swallow, the sentiment rendering me mute for a moment, and nod.

Helena winks. "Bold as brass, remember?"

Heat prickles at my eyes. I do remember.

"And see if you can convince him to visit us, all right?" She grins and backs away. "Or me, at least. Once he's able."

My brows pull together. "What do you mean, once he's able?"

She laughs and spins on a heel, then heads for the forest, waving once without turning around. A loaded pack weights her shoulders, and I imagine Weston must be somewhere out of view, waiting to see her off.

"Once he's able," I murmur to myself. "Once he's able?"

I sigh. Apparently, Helena has more faith in me than I do.

But I can't shake her words, even when night falls and I install myself in the armchair, where I stare into the crackling fire.

Once he's able.

Bold as brass.

The words swoop and dive at me, trailing me to bed and tunneling through my dreams. Hours later, they're still fizzling in the back of my mind when I wake in the darkness to the heavy drone of rain.

I bolt upright, alarm tightening my stomach. It's *pouring*

outside. Rain hits the roof like never-ending scattershot. A chill blankets the room, gnawing at my fingers and toes.

Fortuna, Weston must be freezing.

I jump from bed. Within minutes, I've revived the fire, and the ease with which I do so tells me he hasn't taken refuge in the other room. The moment the flames gain a foothold, I turn from the hearth and sail out the door.

Enough of this. I haven't seen him in over two weeks, and I can't stand it anymore. I won't. I refuse to leave him out there in misery.

Bold as brass.

Outside, night engulfs me, a roar of rain and darkness. I wonder what time it is, how long I have until sunrise—and potential discovery—then decide it doesn't matter. Weston's going to spend the rest of the night inside, my canceled luck be damned. The duke's men won't be out in weather like this, anyway.

"Weston!" I cry, but my holler gets lost the moment it leaves my mouth. I set out across the clearing, then stop and look up.

I should be wet. Only I'm not. Goosebumps prickle on my arms and frigid air eddies beneath my nightgown, chilling me in uncomfortable places, but not a single raindrop touches me. Falling water batters the grass around me, but I stand amid an oasis of stormlessness.

I take a step left. So does the dry spot.

I step right. Same thing.

I sigh and drag my hands down my face, hating that I'm dry when Weston is undoubtedly soaked, but then it hits me.

I can find him this way. I only have to wander until I get wet. Then I'll know he's mere feet away, nullifying my luck.

I set out into the pitch-dark forest. The scent of wet pine stings my nose while springy bracken dampens my bare soles, but I keep dry. Cold and half-lost, maybe, but dry.

A dozen times, I shout Weston's name. Nothing answers but the fury of the storm. Occasional lightning flashes in the distance, but by the time the resultant thunder reaches me, it's more vibration than sound.

And then...

Plop. A bead of ice hits my skin. Then another. Plop. Plop.

I peer around. The cabin's window has shrunk to a watery pinpoint behind me. In every direction, rain sheets off pine boughs. Nothing distinguishes this place from any other. "Weston?"

No reply. The rain bellows.

I take another step, and suddenly, I'm drenched. The rain hits me like an assault, a shower of icy bullets fired from above. My nightgown soaks through in an instant.

I barely register the shock of cold, except to note that Weston has been enduring this for hours. At the realization, my desperation grows. I shout his name again. Nothing.

Then I spot a shape in the darkness ahead, huddled against the trunk of a pine.

My heart seizes.

It's him. It has to be.

Chapter Fifteen

"**W**eston!" I dart forward. He lifts his head at my approach, and even in the dimness, I can tell he's drenched, his hair plastered to his forehead, water streaming in rivulets down his face. He's shivering. Violently.

Even so, some tangled knot inside me loosens at the sight of him.

"B-Birdie?" His teeth chatter around the word. "What're you d-doing out here?"

"Looking for you." I drop to my knees beside him, heedless of the mud and bracken. My hands flutter like pale moths in the darkness, but I don't touch him. Not for lack of wanting to, but because he isn't wearing his gloves, and his black sleeves have ridden up well past his wrists.

I glance around. A sodden sleeping pallet lies nearby, along with a few scattered clothes, no more than wet, dark puddles amid other wet, dark puddles. A collection of pine boughs creates a lean-to against the tree trunk, but the branches slump, their integrity clearly having given way at some point in the last few hours.

Just his luck.

I turn back to him. "You can't stay out here. You're freezing."

"I'm f-f-fine." Tremors wrack his frame.

Fortuna's blessings. This stubborn ass.

"You're definitely not." I crawl over to the pallet and hunt around until I come up with his gloves. They're sopping wet, the cotton lining so waterlogged I can barely jam my fingers in, but I manage. I grab his arm and haul him upright with a strength borne of determination. "You need to come warm up by the fire."

He resists. "I c-can't.... The duke's m-m-men..."

"Won't be out in this storm. And I won't let you catch your death out here."

He hesitates, but another full-body shudder saps him of the will to protest. I haul on his arm, and we stagger through the downpour together, back to the welcoming light of the cabin.

Inside, I steer him to the armchair by the now-roaring fire. He collapses into it, dripping everywhere, quaking with cold.

"Take off your clothes," I order.

That snaps him out of his hypothermic daze. Gold sparks fly in his eyes, though he refuses to look at me. "What? N-no."

"Yes. You're never going to warm up with all that wet fabric sticking to you."

His brows snap low, and the sight of his familiar indignation swims through my veins like warm syrup. He's going to be okay. I just have to get him out of those damn clothes.

"It's not like I haven't seen a naked man before," I say. "Or have you forgotten?"

He leans away, his nostrils flaring. "Forgotten? No. I've t-tried. And tried. It d-doesn't seem to have worked."

I pause, already regretting bringing up Theodore. Then again... "Well, I don't exactly love knowing you've been with a whole bunch of women, either, but we'll both survive. *If* we can get you dry."

His jaw hardens, muting the clatter of his teeth. "There weren't *that* many. W-women. And they all looked like you. Every single one."

Whatever response I might have given to that lodges in my throat. I'm not sure I wanted to know that, backhanded compliment that it is.

"Sorry." His voice is still unsteady, but gaining strength as warmth seeps into him. "I didn't need to share that."

"No. You didn't. Now take your clothes off."

Thank the goddess, he doesn't argue this time. He curls forward and works his sodden shirt over his head before throwing it aside. It hits the floorboards with a wet squish. Then he's rising from the chair, unbuttoning his breeches with stiff fingers and stepping free. He tosses those away, too.

He straightens. He's left his underwear on, but I barely register that fact, because my whole body has been reduced to a hungry ache.

Fortuna help me. He's excruciatingly, glaringly beautiful. Even stippled in goosebumps, he makes my eyes hurt and my mouth go dry.

The funny thing is, I've seen it all before. I've memorized the exact curve of his triceps, how the muscle flexes and contracts when he lashes out with a right hook. I know the precise breadth of his shoulders, the angle at which they join his neck. I'm familiar with the rise of his collarbones and the serrated grooves overlying his ribcage, the vee of muscle that leads downward into his sodden shorts. Even the corded length of his thighs ceased to be a mystery to me long ago.

But I've only ever seen those things in flashes before, and in the company of a crowd. Not laid out in cohesive splendor like this. Not lit by private firelight, in a room that suddenly feels much too small, nestled within a forest that now feels much too large.

I look. And look. A low, liquid flutter beats in my belly.

Weston glares at the floor, apparently ignorant to the silent, irreparable toppling of every daydream I've ever entertained. Because I've thought about him so many times, at night in my bedroom. I've reconstructed what I've seen in the ring so endlessly, inside the privacy of my own head.

But this... This is better.

He finally glances up. His hair curves over his forehead, a perfect crescent.

A hiss staggers in through his lips. "Birdie, you're..." The rest is garbled, but it sounds like a curse.

He abruptly lifts his eyes to the ceiling and presses a fist to his mouth. The other cups his groin, which looks...larger than it did a moment ago.

I furrow my brow, then glance down at myself and—

Oh.

The rain has transformed the thin silk of my nightgown to diaphanous gauze. The soaked fabric does nothing to hide the hard pink peaks of my nipples, or the dark patch nestled at the juncture of my thighs. The gown molds to my every curve while my hair trails over my shoulders in snaking rivers.

Weston wedges a curled forefinger between his teeth. He bites down and studies the ceiling like it holds the secrets to all existence. "You need to put something on. Something that's...not that."

I sweep my gaze down the length of him, lingering on the swell in his shorts. I can't tell if he's shielding or gripping himself, but whatever he's doing, it drives the potent throb in my belly deeper.

That reaction is for me. Because of *me*.

Bold as brass.

"No," I say.

He jerks his gaze down to mine. Once there, he can't seem to help himself. His eyes drift lower, then lower still, lingering on every dip and swell.

It's like being painted with fire. I let my hands hang loose at my sides, my fingers flexing inside his saturated gloves. I'm so cold, yet I'm burning up. Being incinerated from the inside out by the heated weight of his stare.

"This is warfare," he says through a dry, cracked throat. "You *have* to put clothes on."

I raise my chin. "No. I...like you looking at me."

Shadows pile into his eyes. "Fortuna, you're going to keep at this, aren't you? Until you win. Until you break me."

Agreement flies to the tip of my tongue, but I bite down. This isn't fair. I know that. And I promised myself that if we ever did this—truly did this—it would be his choice.

Which I'll hold myself to. I *will*.

But that doesn't mean I can ignore the ravenous throb between my thighs.

"I won't ask you to touch me again," I say, feeling my way through what I'm trying to communicate. "I'll promise you, even. *If* you can promise me something in return."

A swallow grinds down his throat. I can *feel* the difficulty he has keeping his eyes on mine. His struggle boils in the air. "What's that?"

"Stop walking away from me," I say. "Stop leaving. I hate it, and I don't want you to do it ever again. I don't care if we fight. If we...disagree. But from now on, I want you to stay and talk to me about it. I'll stop asking you to touch me, if you'll just stop leaving."

A muscle ticks in his jaw. The fire's crackle swells to fill the silence. I can practically hear the gears turning in his head as he grapples with himself.

But Helena was right. He's teetering, I can see it. Part of him wants to give in. Another part still believes he's no good for me. That I'm better off without him.

He just needs a push. Or maybe a good, hard shove.

"Please." I pour every ounce of myself into the word, until it's more than merely heartful. It's a confession. "I've hated being away from you these past weeks. I'm no good at it. At not having you in my life."

His face is unreadable, but his dangling hand clenches at his side. After a long moment, he says, "It's not exactly my forte, either. I almost came back. So many times, I almost came back."

Something bright and sweet flickers in my chest. It takes me a moment to place it, but when I do, I yield to a shaky smile. Hope. "Then do. For the love of Fortuna, stop staying away from me."

Long moments crawl by, the tension thickening with each passing second. Just when I think he's going to bolt again, he expels a shuddering breath. "I can only do that if you stop asking me to touch you. To kiss you. Because it's torture,

Birdie. You don't understand what it does to me. How cruel you're being when you ask."

My breath catches. I…hadn't thought of it that way. "I won't, then. Not ever again."

A beat passes. "Is that a promise?"

I swallow and force a nod. It's easier than making the vow out loud.

After a long moment, he says, "Okay. Okay, then. I'll stay."

A slow breath leaks out of me. Thank the goddess. "Okay. All right. Thank you. Now will you sit down?"

His face pulls into a frown. "What? Why?"

"Because. I want to see you. I want to look at you. I want…" Something heady and dazzling slides into my mind. "I want to try something."

Wariness hardens his features. "What kind of something?"

"You'll see."

The sharply etched lines of his body all tighten in synchrony, but after long seconds of contemplation, he does as I ask. He lowers himself into the armchair, one hand still shielding his groin. He's almost too large for the seat, his size rendering the thing ridiculous.

But the chair is probably sturdier than it looks. Sturdy enough to take the both of us.

I hope.

"Put your hands on the arms," I say.

His eyes darken. "Birdie," he says, a warning.

I wave the word away, though I can scarcely say where all this assertiveness is coming from. Probably the same place that hoards the words he spoke to me the other night. *I love you so much, and want you so badly, that I can't see anything else, sometimes.*

"I'm not going to touch you," I say. "Not directly, at least."

"Just…indirectly?"

"Yes. But nothing that risks our Marks. I swear it."

He chews on that, then grudgingly spreads his arms and clamps his fingers around the armrests. He splays his knees, putting himself on full display. And…

My tongue thickens, growing heavy in my mouth. He's beautiful everywhere. Thick and lovely where he strains against his sodden shorts.

When he catches me staring, something new kindles in his eyes. It almost looks like a challenge, and I realize how right he was—this is warfare. Flat out. But hopefully the kind where we both can win.

I step closer. I end up standing between his spread legs, my silk-clad knees bumping against the cushion. I stare down into honeyed, half-lidded eyes.

For a moment, neither of us moves. The air threatens to combust. Weston's gaze wanders, carving a blazing path down my body.

I shiver and reach for his wrist, closing my gloved fingers around it. I lift his hand and set it against the curve of my waist.

He stems an inhale. So do I.

"See?" I manage, once I recover from the shock. "We're not touching."

He stares at where his hand molds to the swell of my hip. His palm is broad and rough, and gives off heat as if the drenched silk separating us isn't even there.

I release his wrist, but his hand stays in place. After a breathless moment, he lifts the other to collar my waist in his grip.

He hesitates. Then tugs.

I pitch forward, ending up with my hands braced against the chairback, my forearms inches from his ears. He tips his face up and searches mine. My wet hair drapes around him.

He shapes a velvety curse. "This is what you wanted to show me?"

"Yes."

"Touching without touching?"

"Yes."

"This is dangerous," he says. "This is crazy." But I *have* him, because in the next moment, his hands start to roam.

Fire curls and coils around the base of my spine. Goddess, Weston is touching me. Weston Wildes is *touching me*, and it's every bit as heady and inebriating as I thought it would be.

He traces my curves through my nightgown, running his thumbs over my stomach, exploring the outside of my thighs, brushing the backs of his fingers up along my front.

"More," I whimper. "Everywhere you can."

His eyes flash, and he palms my breasts, testing their weight.

A needy whine slips out of me. He responds with a guttural sound and pinches each nipple, rolling them through his fingers. Sensation zaps into me, a lightning bolt that touches down between my legs.

And I can't help myself. I climb into a straddle atop him.

He stiffens as my knees settle beside his hips. But my nightgown sheathes me from ankle to collar. The only part of me left bare is my arms, which I keep angled away.

"Still not touching," I whisper.

He mutters a curse and gathers me closer, apparently emboldened by the protective layer between us. "We shouldn't be doing this," he says, but his hands are everywhere now, dragging worshipful strokes down my flanks, tracing shivers up my spine, settling around my ass and squeezing. He gazes up at me, eyes glinting, and says a very filthy word. Then his grip settles at my hips. He yanks me close, pulling my most intimate places flush against his.

My eyes widen at the contact. He tilts my pelvis, coaxing it into a roll, and I gasp. Pleasure spirals through me, silver-tipped and sparkling.

I squeeze out a few desperate words. "Oh. Oh, my goddess."

He searches my eyes. "Do you feel me?"

"Yes," I gasp. No way could I not. "But I think you should take off your shorts."

I don't want a single layer between us that doesn't need to be there.

I know how far gone he is now because he doesn't even argue. I raise my body just enough that he can wedge his hands between us and shimmy his underwear off, and then he's settling me against him again, notching the hard ridge of his desire into the exact right place. He guides my hips into another undulation, gifting me with delicious friction.

Then another.

A moan flutters up my throat as my head falls back and my eyes close. I want to look at him, want to map the taut lines of him, how they move beneath me, but I can't manage. I can only squeeze the chairback tighter as a thrum of pleasure builds in my solar plexus. I arch and flex, arch and flex, steered by his capable hands.

"Bria." He rasps my name on a broken exhale. "Goddess, I missed you. I missed you so much I could barely breathe."

I shudder. This time, I love that he didn't call me Birdie. This time, it feels like he's giving me my name as a gift.

"Me, too," I say, and roll my pelvis, grinding against him, the silk between us so thin as to be meaningless. He guides me in a way that must please him as much as it does me, because his breathing whittles down to short, hard gasps.

I'm wet. Slippery. I'm falling and flying, both at once. I buck against him, beholden to the press of him between my legs, to the way he fits against me so perfectly. My belly pulls taut. Bliss gathers everything tight, tight, tight, and goddess, I could come like this.

I'm going to.

I pry my lashes apart and gaze down my cheeks at him. His lips are parted, his eyes reflecting the firelight, his beauty stark and violent and humbling.

"Can you..." I gasp out, "...finish like this?"

"Yes." The word sounds so raw and unarmored it's like he's reached down and pulled it up from some borderless place within himself. "Easily. Can you?"

I choke out an affirmative. My hips churn faster. Euphoria uncages itself in my core and rockets outward along every nerve. Close. I'm so close. Fortuna, I wish I could touch him. Kiss him.

Then I remember I'm still wearing his gloves. I force my grip from the chairback and resettle my hands atop the rounded musculature of his shoulders.

He lifts his chin, baring his throat. "Squeeze."

Surprise flickers, but the roar building inside me drowns it out. I slide my fingers around his neck and do as he asks.

His eyes roll up in his head. He pulls me harder against him, and suddenly I'm cresting the pinnacle, needy noises flying from my throat as my eyes slam closed and my body detonates inward.

Sensation pours through me in glittering waterfalls. They swell and ebb and swell again.

I fly apart into beautiful pieces. And Weston is clearly doing the same, because he's all hoarse cries and straining muscle as he wraps his arms around my waist and hangs on. His hips flex up off the chair as he surges against me, finding his release.

When the tidal crash of pleasure finally relaxes its grip, I go limp. My hands fall from his throat. I catch my breath in silence, my fingers trailing downward to frame his triquetra.

His Mark regards me like a triple eye. Squinting. Suspicious.

I stare at where my bare wrists hover an inch from his skin. An inch. Just one. That's all it would take. It would be *so* easy.

But I cast the thought aside and force my eyes upward.

Weston's head lolls back against the cushion. He looks...dazed. Drunk. "That was..."

I brace for something I don't want to hear. *Good enough,* maybe. Or, *nice, but not completely satisfying.*

"...the best thing that's ever happened to me," he finishes. "That was the highest point of my entire life."

I blink. "Really? Even though it's not as much as you've done with—"

"Birdie." He lifts his head, shaking some of the haze from his eyes. "They were nothing. Just stand-ins for you. And poor ones, at that."

Something tender awakens at the base of my throat—some fragile, featherless emotion I want so fiercely to protect.

"And I always had to rush through," he adds. "I've never just...enjoyed it."

I hold his eyes. He holds mine.

"Thank you," he murmurs.

And there they are again, those two words, in all their simplistic glory.

"Thank *you*," I say, after a beat. "That was the highest point of my life, too."

A ghost of a smile touches his mouth before he suppresses it. I almost get lost in the way he's looking at me, because I want to exist here forever, in this tenuous peace we've forged with our bodies. I want this moment to stretch and stretch and never end.

Eventually, though, it does. It has to. I climb off him, acutely aware that my nightgown is sticky and even wetter than before. He sprawls bonelessly in the chair, his release glistening on his skin, and I squash the desire to kneel before him. I want to drag my tongue across the ridges of his abdomen, find out what he tastes like.

I hate that I never will. That I promised I wouldn't.

But *that*, what we just did... I'd do that a thousand times over again, if he'd let me.

"It could be like this every night, you know," I say softly. "You and me. Together but apart. We could make it work. And you'd never have to rush, with me. You wouldn't have to worry."

He blinks once, long and—I dare to think—considering. It's clear that what we just shared has torn away some of his shields, because there's no guardedness in his voice when he says, "I love you. So much that I don't know what to do with myself sometimes. And... Fortuna, I can't believe I'm saying this, but I'd love nothing more than to marry you and have you swan around this cabin wearing a soaked nightgown all the time."

I hold my breath, sensing there's more. "But?"

He grinds his molars together. "But... *But*...even if you agreed to do it my way, even if you promised to keep your Mark forever, Brendan would never allow it. I knew that when I proposed. I've always known. As long as you have your triquetra, you're destined for someone richer and more influential than I'll ever be."

The air cools, even though the flames haven't lessened. "So that's...what? That's it? That's okay with you?"

"No," he says, with a trace of his usual fire. "Of course not. I hate it. But that doesn't mean I can change the rules."

"But you know Brendan's only marrying me to Alverton for his own sake."

He chews on that for a moment. "Yes. And part of me hates him for that. Even though he's my best friend."

"But why?" The shrillness of my tone surprises me. "Why do you still think of him that way when he denied you? When he's so...selfish? Greedy?"

Weston sighs, but doesn't break from my gaze, like he usually does. That simple fact tells me we've surpassed some barrier. A new trust expands between us, soft and fresh, like the newly unfurled wings of a butterfly, poised to harden in the sun.

"Because there've been three people in my life," he says, "who've treated me like I matter. One of them is you."

He props his elbow on the armrest and ticks off names on his fingers. "The second is Helena. Your brother's the third. So, yes, Brendan may be selfish. And greedy. But he wasn't always that way. And he's one of the only people I've ever been able to just *exist* with. Everyone else stays away, and it's better like that, but him...he was always different. Maybe because he had a Charm for a sister, and could afford to spend time with a Null without suffering for it, but he was my friend when friends were a luxury I couldn't afford. And that means something to me. More than I can put into words."

Whatever retort I had planned deserts me. I can't argue with that. I would never presume to deny him what he considers his sole true friendship.

"Okay. I think I get it." And I do. "But...that doesn't mean we have to listen to him. We could get married on our own and tell him afterward. He'd have no choice but to deal with it, then. My parents, too, if they ever come home. And that's the only way the duke's men will stop coming for me. The only way out of this that doesn't involve me marrying Alverton."

His mouth flattens to a thoughtful line, and my heart lifts. Fortuna's blessings, he's actually thinking about it.

"Is that really what you want?" he finally says. "To marry someone who can never fully please you?"

"You pleased me just now." The words tumble out. "That was..." *Everything Theodore couldn't manage*, I almost say.

Weston's lips twist, as if I've made the declaration out loud.

I swallow and change tacks. "Incredible. Even better than I'd hoped. And trust me, I'd hoped. Endlessly. And also, I love you. In the permanent, branded-on-my-soul kind of way. I love you so much that I'd gladly take just half of you over the entirety of any other man."

His eyes widen, and then he closes them, as if basking in

that. When he refocuses on me, he looks faintly awestruck. "I never dreamed I'd actually hear you say that to me."

I make a soft, plaintive sound. "I've been wanting to say it for ten years. It's been true, all that time."

A wealth of emotion passes over his face—nearly every feeling I can put a name to, except anger.

His fingers tap rhythmically against the chair. "If we did this..."

Every muscle in my body winds tight. He's actually talking about this. Considering this. I can scarcely believe it.

"...it *would* solve some problems. Problems I don't have any other solution to."

My heart takes a flying leap into my throat.

"I'd be able to protect you," he says. "From the duke, at least. And from Brendan's bad decision-making."

"Yes." The word comes out as a cry, so freighted with joy I'm surprised it doesn't break in half. "You could."

"But..." He searches my face. "You couldn't ever touch me. You understand that, right? You'd have to keep your promise. Because I'm only so strong. It's taken everything I had just to stay away from you these past weeks."

That tender thing in my throat swells and hums. "Yes. Okay. I could do that. If it meant being your wife."

Hope and hesitation mingle in his eyes. "Maybe I should've considered the upsides of wet nightgowns earlier. It just... didn't occur to me that it would ever be an option."

My laugh comes out half-sob. Something is happening. A future is coming to life around us, like spring blooms pushing through the snow after a long, lean winter. The room lightens and brightens and wraps me in warmth.

"You know, when I built this place," he says quietly, "I didn't actually plan to wall these rooms off."

I suck down an inhale. He looks taken aback, like he's already shocked by what he's about to say.

I hold still. I don't dare interrupt.

"I...meant to build an open archway," he says haltingly. "But on the day I went to do it, I just kept mortaring. Stone after stone. A whole wall. Solid. And when I stepped back to look, I felt like an idiot. Because I knew exactly what I'd done, and why. Deep down, I dreamed of having you here. You on your side, me on mine. Together but apart. Like you said."

My throat tightens. The fact that he's imagined a life with me, even if we can never join in the way we both crave, sets my soul ablaze.

"Together but apart," I whisper.

His brow creases. "Would that really be enough for you? *Can* it be?"

"Yes." It's absolutely enough. It's everything.

"You'd have to be sure. Completely."

"I am." No hesitation.

He chews on his lip. Silence presses in from all sides, and I hold my breath. Whatever he says next will decide everything.

"Then..." He pauses, as if trying his answer out in his head before giving it. "I guess I should propose. Again."

I take a second to process the words. When their meaning settles, joy floods me, preserving the moment in perfect diamond clarity. This time, there's no coercion, no desperation. Just Weston and I choosing each other, of our own free will.

"Yes." I can barely get the word out, it's so loaded with

SHAYLIN GANDHI

wonder. "That's your answer. Yes. Forever yes. You don't even have to ask."

A telltale glint rises in his eyes. But he clears his throat and pulls himself to standing. He comes close and peers down, and he's so...pure right now. Unadorned. More himself than he's ever allowed me to see before.

"I'd choose half of you, too," he says. "I'd choose your little toe, even. Over any other woman."

Emotion rushes up my throat. I long to rise on tiptoes and feather my mouth against his. It would be safe, probably, if it only lasted a moment. But I crush the urge in a ruthless fist, because I made a promise. One I won't break. Besides, this will be my life, now—resisting him. At least until the day he changes his mind.

If he ever does.

"We'll go tomorrow?" he says. "And put an end to this idea of you marrying Alverton?"

"Tomorrow," I agree, my heart bursting into song. "Where?"

"One town over. Ravenfell. No one will know us there. As long as we cover our Marks."

"Yes. Anywhere." My gaze falls to his mouth. It's a beautiful mouth, as sharply defined as the rest of him. "I can't wait."

He smiles. It's small but genuine, and I can't believe that this whole time, all I had to do was promise never to touch him.

"Get some rest," he says. "All right?"

Words fail me. I nod.

He looks like he wants to reach for me, but he doesn't, of course. "I wish we didn't need a wall between us. But I don't trust myself without one. I'd probably find my way from my bed to yours in my sleep. Do something that can't be undone, without even meaning to."

I manage another nod.

"So I'll see you in the morning, Birdie. All right?"

"All right."

A moment later, he's tugging on his underwear and gathering his clothes. He slips out the door, closing it softly behind him, and I stand in the flickering firelight, my arms wrapped around myself. On the far side of the wall, Weston bustles around. The sounds fill my ears like a symphony.

Together but apart. And tomorrow, I'll be his wife. We'll pledge our lives to one another, even if we can never touch.

It might be less than I wanted, and it'll mean keeping my luck for the rest of my life, but it's more than I've ever had before. And as long as we're together, nullifying each other's magic, maybe I can save him from an early end. He'll even be able to sleep at night, safe on the other side of that wall.

He'll be mine, as much as he can be.

Gratitude soaks into me, so complete it eclipses any shred of doubt. I fall into bed with a smile on my face.

My dreams that night are spun from sunbeams, glowing and golden.

Chapter Sixteen

I awake with the first rays of dawn, my heart a soft, bright thing in my chest. Today, I'll become Bria Wildes. By the time the sun sets, I'll be Weston's wife.

It's almost too beautiful to be real.

I yield to a dreamy smile, too contented to get out of bed yet. Silence blankets the room, and I picture Weston still lost to slumber, enjoying his very first night of uninterrupted sleep. For long minutes, I bask in the knowledge that I was able to give that to him. But soon, a growing urge overtakes me.

I want to do something more for him. Something to reciprocate all he's done for me. Something specific, like the hairbrush.

How many options do I have, though, out here in the woods?

I think until my brain hurts, then settle on an idea. Soundlessly, I slip from bed and tug on a simple yellow dress, then grab my wicker gathering basket. As quietly as I can, I ease the door open and emerge into the morning.

The rain has stopped. In the forest, dew limns the foliage in silver, and I strike out toward the trees.

At the edge of the clearing, I hesitate. Weston probably wouldn't like me venturing out alone like this, what with the duke's men still searching. But as long as we're separated, my luck will protect me. No one will find me unless I want them to.

And I'll be quick.

With that decided, I wend my way into the woods, in search of flowers to weave into a bridal crown. I plan on making a matching boutonniere for Weston's lapel—a small gesture, but one laden with meaning. It'll be a symbol of unity. A way for us to touch when our hands can't.

The forest grows thicker. Branches tug at my skirts, but I press onward. I don't know what kind of bloom I'm looking for, only that I'll recognize it when I see it.

A flash of color catches my eye, and I push aside a screen of foliage. A gasp escapes me.

There, in a clearing, grows some kind of wildflower I've never encountered before. Star-shaped blossoms gleam in the dawn, their golden petals ruffling on a phantom breeze.

I step closer. The find is beyond lucky—so few wild-flowers bloom this late in the season, and these happen to be the exact color of Weston's hair.

Golden flowers for my golden boy. A gift from Fortuna, if I ever saw one.

A smile spreads as I kneel in the grass. The sweet, delicate fragrance tickles my nose as I gather the blossoms for my basket.

Lost as I am in my task, I almost miss the sounds behind me.

But then a twig cracks, making me freeze. Weston. It has to be. No one else could have found me. I pivot and peer over my shoulder.

Fear douses me in ice. It's not Weston.

A stranger stands a few feet away, his hands folded, a black tricorn shadowing steel-gray eyes. His maroon greatcoat is fine, edged in gold braid that winks in the dawn.

For a moment, I can only gape. How'd he get here?

A slow smile curls his lips. "Hello, Bria."

My tongue cleaves to the roof of my mouth. Fortuna help me, this isn't good. The fact that he knows my name is a very, very bad sign.

"Bria? Who's Bria?" I try.

He smirks. "Let's not do any of that, now. It'd only be a waste of time."

My heart thumps a staccato rhythm against my ribs. Okay, next tactic. "Did the duke send you? Because I can top whatever he's paying you. I can make it worth your while to walk away."

"Maybe you could," he says impassively. "But Ramses didn't come here for money. He's rich already. Now he just likes to do the impossible. Find people who don't want to be found."

I jerk a glance around, scanning for a second man. "Ramses? Who's Ramses? Is he—"

"Right here. You're looking at him."

I swing widened eyes back to the intruder. "You...talk about yourself in the third person?"

He laughs, but there's something wrong with it. It comes out too high, too fast, and my hope fractures with a sad, snapping sound.

I do my best to cling to the broken pieces. Weston will come. Any moment now, my luck will rear its head and put a stop to what's unfolding.

"Don't bother waiting for it," Ramses says. "It won't save you."

"What won't?"

"Your Mark."

The air in my lungs thins to a whisper. "What? Why not?"

His smile widens. "Because. Ramses is lucky, too." He reaches up and tugs his cravat away from his throat. And there, in stark relief, is a familiar three-pointed knot. A triquetra, black as jet.

He's...Marked. Oh, goddess.

"You're a Charm," I rasp.

"Mmm-hmm. And when the Charm wants to find you, find you he does. Ramses walked straight to you."

My pulse skips and stutters. This can't be happening. "Stay away from me."

To my horror, he steps closer. "Don't make this too hard on yourself, now. Ramses doesn't like being forceful with women."

I scramble backwards, flowers tumbling from my frozen fingers, the basket thudding into the grass. I open my mouth to scream, but he lunges forward and seizes my wrist.

At the touch, a shock of sensation lances into my arm, like the buzz of a thousand bees trapped beneath my skin. A high-pitched whine builds in my ears.

Fortuna, I've never touched another Charm before, and I don't like it. At all.

Pain engulfs me. The last thing I see before darkness

claims me is a pair of quicksilver eyes, glinting with exultation.

Chapter Seventeen

Awareness trickles in, layer by layer.

My head pounds. Every inch of me feels raw and scalded, like I've been dipped in acid and hung out on the line to dry.

I peel my eyes open for the second time today.

Except this awakening feels nothing like the first. The hope that buoyed me this morning has vanished, leaving me bereft. Because wherever I am right now, it's somewhere Weston's not.

Shadows crowd the room. A single candle glows on a table, but I can't tell whether it's noon or midnight, because there are no windows. At least whatever bed I've been dumped into is plush, the bedding luxurious.

I struggle into a sit. My stomach dips and sways, but I manage to hold it still after a few resolute swallows.

Then I shriek and flinch back. A man sits at the foot of the bed, regarding me with mild eyes.

"Alverton," I manage.

"Miss Bria." The duke is immaculately dressed, his hair

brushed back with precision. He's every bit as handsome as I remember. "I trust you enjoyed your journey?"

I blink. Is he serious? My eyes dart, taking measure of my surroundings. We must be on his estate, because the furnishings are lavish. A gilt-trimmed wardrobe stands against one wall. A wedding dress hangs from its door, even more extravagant than the one I wore into the woods.

I hate it on sight.

"Hmm," Alverton says. "Not as vocal as you were last month, it seems."

I inch back until my spine presses against the headboard. A rustle in the corner claims my attention, and I startle all over again.

Ramses lurks in the shadows, his arms crossed, his tricorn pulled low.

"Well, no matter." The duke's gaze is serene. "I don't actually need you to talk. I only need you to put on that dress." He gestures to the wardrobe. "As soon as the ceremony's complete, you'll accompany me to my office. I have some contracts that need signing. Entrepreneurial ventures you'll need to ensure the success of. I've already put them on hold for far too long."

I huddle into the pillows, wishing I could disappear. "No. No, that's not going to happen. I'm sorry, but..." My tongue trips over itself. Why did I just apologize? I didn't mean that in the slightest.

I gather a breath and try again. "I'm promised to someone else. It's been decided. I'm marrying him, not you."

The duke's laugh holds genuine amusement. "Let me guess, that Null ruffian from your foyer? Go ahead. Marry him. I'll only bring you right back here again. Because I was promised a Charmed wife, and that's what I'm getting. As far as I'm concerned, you're already bought and paid for."

Indignation blooms hot in my chest. "You can't just *buy* people."

"Can't I?" He spreads his hands. "My contract with your brother would suggest I can."

Brendan. Just thinking his name makes me want to scream. "I never agreed to that."

"But your family did," he says, all confidence. "And soon enough, so will you."

I shake my head, my heartbeat a trapped, frantic thing in my throat. "I won't. I want to go home."

"Miss Bria, you're already there."

Words fail me, the sheer assuredness in his expression withering my anger to dust. Tears spring to my eyes. This has all gone so horribly wrong. As if my luck doesn't even exist. Maybe it doesn't, with another Charm in the room. Or maybe Ramses' luck outranks mine, somehow.

"You're fortunate," the duke continues, placid. "Most husbands aren't as lenient as I am. Most would wonder what you were doing with that highwayman, out there in the woods. Most would wonder why, when you found yourself alone, you chose to pick flowers instead of fleeing your captor."

Wariness prickles along my skin.

"It's enough to wonder if your Null lover and the man who stole you had anything in common."

I clamp my teeth together, fear stitching my lips closed. I'll die before giving Weston up.

But Alverton only chuckles. "Oh, Miss Bria, you're far less clever than you realize. But I couldn't care less about what you two did out there. You still have your Mark. That's all that matters. And once we're married, I'm willing to put this all behind us. You'll spend your days in my office and your nights in my bed, and we'll consider your past just that. That's more than generous of me, I think."

Bile rises in my throat, hot and stinging. "You can't force me to marry you."

"Oh, I have no intention of *forcing* you. I'm going to wait until you ask."

I bare my teeth. "That'll never happen."

"I doubt that very much. Because there's only one way you're leaving this room."

All the blood drains from my cheeks. "What?"

"This"—he gestures around—"is your world now. At least until you put on that dress."

A whimper claws its way out of me. "What? No. You can't keep me here forever."

"No, I imagine not." Alverton stands and brushes imaginary lint from his lapel. "You'll probably get thirsty after a day or so."

My mouth falls open. "Thirsty? What, you're going to keep me here without food? Without *water?*"

His lips quirk. "Your change of heart will be a quick one, I think. Just put on that dress once you've decided, and we can move forward. I'll check in on you tomorrow, all right?"

My fingers curl into the sheets, clawlike. He can't be serious. He can't mean to imprison me here.

The duke strides to the door and opens it. "And in case you're banking on your luck saving you, it won't. No amount of kismet can unlock four deadbolts. Which is exactly what's on the other side of this door."

My throat thickens. I try to wall off the tears, but they overflow without my permission, carving hot paths down my cheeks. "You can't do this. My brother—"

"Thinks you're still lost in the woods. And will continue to do so until you've become my wife."

I fist the sheets so hard my hands ache. "No. Just…use Ramses. You don't even need me."

The duke raises an eyebrow.

I glare at the man who snatched me from the woods. From my almost-happiness. "Take *him* to your office. Use his luck to sign your contracts."

Alverton sighs. "Oh, Miss Bria. Ramses is only a procurer. Now that you've been procured, he's off to his next job. Besides, you and me should establish our routine sooner rather than later, don't you think?"

My limbs go numb and heavy. Dread settles over me like a shroud.

"Don't argue with him, pet," Ramses says.

I hiss at him. "You. Why're you even helping him?"

"Because." He peers at his fingernails and shrugs. "Ramses said so already. He likes to do what no one else can."

"You're evil," I say, but the sob that ruptures my voice halfway through robs the accusation of power. "I knew it the moment you touched me."

He smiles in a way that makes my skin crawl. "Hurts the first time, doesn't it? All that luck in one place. It's like shoving two positive sides of a magnet together. But the sting…" His voice drops to a purr. "It starts to feel good, the more times you do it. Ramses likes it now. You should try it again, some time."

My tears flow faster. I wonder if he was always mad, or if

something about touching other Charms made him that way. "You've lost your mind."

"Maybe." His grin slashes white in the dimness. "But right now, Ramses suggests you be a good girl and put on that wedding dress. Fighting will only make it worse for you."

"Wise words," Alverton adds from the doorway.

My chest burns itself to ashes. I want to scream. To rage. To rend the fear and hopelessness brewing inside me to ribbons.

The duke clicks his tongue. Ramses tips his hat to me, then strolls out.

"This is wrong," I shout through my sobs. "This is inhumane."

Alverton lingers in the doorway. His eyes are impassive, almost fond. "No, my dear. This is business."

The door closes with a click of finality.

Chapter Eighteen

I don't know how much time passes.

At first, I wander the room, hunting for something I can fashion into a lockpick, or for a forgotten, hidden passageway that might grant me an escape.

But beneath the gilt and gaudiness, the chamber proves oddly sterile, the furnishings restricted to a bed and wardrobe and table. And a chamberpot, which is inconveniently fashioned from ceramic and therefore useless for trying to smash open the door with.

Every drawer I search is empty. Aside from the wedding dress, the wardrobe proves bare, too. It's as if the place was scoured clean before being repurposed as a prison. Probably by Ramses himself, because anything that might grant my luck a foothold has been removed.

Only another Charm could find every last bauble and leave me with no advantage. His luck has clashed with mine and emerged victorious.

I manage to sleep a little, dreaming fitfully. Some time later—it's morning again, I suppose—the duke strides in.

When he sees me hunkered in the corner, still in my yellow dress, he shakes his head and promises to check again tomorrow.

I turn my face away as the door closes. My throat burns. Time stretches, endless and taunting.

After another hour or five, I try the door. I jiggle the handle a thousand times, until someone on the other side shouts at me to give it a rest. I have a guard, apparently, which comes as no surprise—even with four deadbolts keeping me in, I *am* a Charm.

But my luck can't conjure opportunity from nothing, and no matter how many times I wrench the door handle, it refuses to give. I throw my body against the wood until bruises bloom on my shoulders.

That doesn't work, either.

Briefly, I consider using the candle to torch the place, but without any windows, I can't see how I'll get out of here alive. I'll probably asphyxiate before anyone even smells smoke.

So I retreat to the bed, where I huddle among the sheets and think about Weston. I consider how close I came, how my outstretched fingers brushed against happiness, if only for a moment, before losing hold again.

The agony of it nearly stops my heart. Yet thoughts of him are the only comfort I have. My throat is a fiery chasm, begging for relief, and to distract myself, I weave stories in my mind. I construct scenes from some imagined life together, an alternate reality in which Weston and I never had triquetras.

If only it were real. If only we'd come into this world unMarked.

Then I could've been happy. I could've been *ordinary*.

I could've been married by now.

As the hours swell and my body drains of moisture, desperation hatches inside me, then grows like a monster. First, it gobbles down the stories I spin. Then, my dreams. Lastly, it swallows any hope that Weston might come.

He'll try, maybe, but his curse will keep him from succeeding. He'll only have a chance if he gets close enough to this room to cancel his curse, which is probably impossible, for a Null.

My stomach gnaws on itself. My throat ignites, and my threadbare hope burns to ash in the fire.

The second time the duke visits, his brows crinkle. He's...frowning, I think. I try to piece together why, but my brain has grown sluggish, my body unresponsive. I lay sideways on the bed and stare, unable to find the wherewithal to lift my head.

"Hmm," he says. "Tomorrow's probably your last chance. I suggest you think long and hard about whether your pride is worth dying for."

He leaves me alone.

I drift.

Some time later—a minute or a year—a woman slips into the room. At first, she appears in stolen snatches, stalking around the edges of my vision. Every time I turn my head, she disappears.

But soon, she grows bolder. She pads through the shadows on quiet feet, licking her lips and crooning about escape. She promises freedom from this room, from the body that's rapidly failing me. From my very existence.

Death, I finally realize. That's her name.

I angle my face away. "Leave me alone."

She chuckles from the shadows, sultry and knowing.

I sleep, and when I wake, I'm alone again. Alverton's command fills the silence, spreading like an inkstain on my mind. I fall into endless ruminations about what I'd die for, whether it's worth never seeing my family again. Weston.

Fortuna help me, Weston.

His name is a scar across my heart. Because if I don't give in, I'll die here, in this room. In this bed. I'll have already laid eyes on him for the final time.

But if I *do* surrender, I'll have a chance, at least. I might spot a head of golden hair from a distance, maybe even run into Weston in town.

At the realization, my resolve wobbles. I'm dangling from a cliff by my fingernails, and one by one, my desolation pries them loose.

Because I'm not him, to look death in the face and snarl in welcome. I'm just me. Bria Radcliffe. The Charm, soft and coddled and delicate.

And now, as I lay dying, I prove it by capitulating. Inch by inch, I yield.

I break.

Fortuna help me, I don't want to die.

With my last shreds of strength, I haul myself from bed. My legs barely work and my arms weigh more than the rest of me combined, and I fall three times on my way to the dress. Everything hurts. I can barely tell up from down.

I crawl the last few feet. My half-dead fingers snag the dress's hem.

Finally, a bit of luck, because the gown slides from the hanger as if leaping into my hands.

I manage to get my yellow dress off. That takes an hour. I put the wedding dress on. That takes two.

I pass out.

When I regain consciousness, panic sets in. Maybe I've missed my chance. I have no idea what time it is, what day it is...

What if the duke has come and gone again?

A sob rips from my abused throat. More follow on its heels, but my tortured body produces no tears. I don't have the water for it. I barely have enough energy to drag myself to the door, where I collapse in a tangle of white brocade and nerveless limbs.

Another year crawls by.

I wait. I float. I fade. I fall.

At long last, the door cracks open. I squeeze my eyes shut, recoiling from the hallway's too-bright light.

The duke's boots scuff against the carpet.

"Please," I say. My plea comes out brittle and cracked, like a dry branch breaking in the heat of summer. "I'll marry you. I *want* to."

"I know," he says. "Even if you didn't, I would've come for you anyway, Birdie."

Chapter Nineteen

That voice.

I open my eyes. Or try. My dried-out lids stick to my eyeballs, and I have to force the movement. On the third attempt, my lashes part with reluctance.

I find myself face-to-face with black boots.

I roll onto my back, my gaze traveling up over black-clad legs. Next comes a black shirt that laces at the neck. Then a mask—black fabric, framing amber eyes that slowly fill with horror.

The most beautiful eyes I've ever seen.

"Jack," I croak. "It's you."

"Birdie?" he bleats. "What happened to you?"

Such a surplus of emotion crushes my insides that I pass out again.

When I come to, it's in snatches. Weston is carrying me, I think, because my head lolls and my ankles bob. The world flickers. I glimpse a door with four stout deadbolts, a keyring jammed into its bottom lock. A long, decadent hallway. A man lying on the carpet, beaten senseless, his face too bloodied to be recognizable—my guard, probably. Whoever he was.

Then we're in a dim, cramped stairwell, some back passage intended for staff to use.

"What did he do to you?" someone is saying, over and over again. The voice sounds enraged, and yet it's safety. It's love. It's home.

"Starved me," I say. "No water."

Darkness comes for me again.

Only—no, we've just gone outside, because when I blink, stars hover overhead, peering at me with concern.

"I'll kill him." A world of fire roars inside Weston's words. "He'll die for this."

"No, don't. He'll..." Fortuna, every syllable strips my throat raw. "Just leave it alone. Your curse. He'll hurt you."

Weston swears, then sets me gently in the gravel and disappears into the darkness. I cry out and reach for him, but he's already back, propping me up, setting something against my lips. Cool, sweet life trickles into my mouth.

I gasp. Then gulp. I guzzle every last drop and ask for more.

"We have to get out of here," he says, low and hurried. "And that's all the water I have, but we'll get you more. Can you stand?"

I try. I fail.

"It's okay, it's okay." I think he's crying now. Someone is. Maybe me. Then I'm being hoisted and gripped, maneuvered into a saddle. I slump, devoid the strength to hold myself up, but in another moment, he's behind me, clamping me close.

We're moving. Thank Fortuna. My eyes flutter closed.

When I open them again some time later, something has

changed. Some hint of vitality glows at the crux of me, planted there by the water I swallowed. When I flex my fingers, they obey. I wiggle my toes. Those work, too.

I'm...alive, it seems. I'm still here.

The steady rhythm of hooves beats beneath me. A comforting wall of muscle buttresses my back, and I lean into it, mindful, even now, not to touch him directly.

Weston's arm flexes tighter around my waist. His lips press against my hair. "I have you. I'm not letting go. You're safe."

"How long?" I rasp.

"Two and a half days." His breath feathers against my ear. "The worst two and a half days of my life. And that's saying something."

A choked sound jams in my throat. A laugh or a sob—I can't tell. "What time is it?"

"Two o'clock in the morning."

The night smears past, a chilly tableau of blue shadows and pulsing stars. Pines whisper to one another, but nothing seems as real as Weston does. He spurs the horse onward, eventually swerving off the road and into the woods. Branches glide from the darkness as he guides our mount through the underbrush.

Before long, we emerge into a clearing. A pool shimmers in the moonlight, as round and shining as a fallen coin.

An exultant cry builds inside me. Water. All the water I could possibly hold. My whole body strains, every inch of me curving toward it. Reaching.

Weston slides from the saddle and lifts me down, his grip strong and sure at my waist.

No sooner have my feet touched earth than I'm staggering toward the pool. When I reach it, I splash straight in.

"Birdie, wait."

I don't. It's bitterly cold but I don't care—I cup my hands and drink. Icy liquid cascades down my throat. It pours over my chin and chest, soaking my dress, rejuvenating my senses.

Weston crashes into the pool with me, his grip catching me around the middle just as I sag. He lets me drink until I'm sated, then hauls me back to shore. We collapse on the grassy bank, where he pulls me across his lap, careful to keep his acres of black fabric between us. He hugs me to his chest and rocks me.

I cry.

I break to pieces and let him catch me, because it all pours out at once—the horror, the fear, the utter helplessness of being locked up and treated as chattel. As less than human.

As a thing.

"I'm sorry," Weston whispers fiercely. His gloved hand strokes my hair while sobs wrack my body. "Curses, I'm so sorry. I should've gotten to you sooner. I *tried* to, Birdie, I swear it. I tried and tried and tried. So many things went wrong, but I just kept going, because I knew that once I got to you, it'd be all right. Only it isn't, is it? Not really."

"You came, though," I choke out between tears. "You're here. We're together."

"I know, but...if I'd been any later, if my curse had interfered any more than it did, you might've—"

He cuts himself off, as sharply as if he's chopped the sentence short with a cleaver. After a long moment, he says, "Alverton didn't hurt you in...other ways, did he? Touch you?"

I know what he's asking. "No. Nothing like that." My tears soak his shirtfront. I sniffle and lift my head, my emotional outpouring finally at a close.

The necessary layers separate us, but he's so near, this bulwark of grit and security. His hair curves down over his forehead, as pale as spun gold in the moonlight. As I gaze up, he tugs off his mask and tosses it into the grass, then sets a gloved hand against my cheek. "I've never wanted to kiss you more than I do right now."

Goddess, I wish he could. But I know he can't, and I'm so drained that I just lie in his arms, soaking up the promise of his embrace.

His eyes never leave mine. "Do you have any idea what you mean to me?"

"No," I whisper. "Tell me."

He sucks in a raggedy breath. "Do you remember the day we met?"

"Of course." I could never forget. "I was in the library. Reading."

"Yes." He forces a grim smile, and I crush the urge to reach for him. I have to be content with this, with being held like this. I promised him.

"You were in the armchair," he says, "with a book. Sitting sideways, with your feet kicked over the arm. No shoes. It was the chair in front of the window, I think, because sunlight was pouring in, collecting in this pool around you. It was like the world was sending me a message. Lighting you up. Demanding I pay attention."

I search his face. I don't remember that. The day we met was gray and rainy, I'm sure of it. I'd only taken refuge in the library because my usual reading spot, the one out on the back terrace, was too waterlogged and drippy to use.

"The funny thing is," Weston continues, "I walked into that room hating you."

He must feel me stiffen, because he makes a soothing sound. "I know, I know, but hear me out. I walked into that room hating you, because Brendan had warned me in advance that he had a Charm for a sister. And I figured I knew you. The whole time he and I were walking out to your house, I couldn't stop thinking about how easy you'd had it. How life was just one big party for you, while I was stuck with the bits no one wanted. You were about to be the only Charm I'd ever met, and I felt like you'd stolen something from me, on some personal level. Like Fortuna had taken my luck and given it to you, before we were even born."

A squeak emerges, the front end of a protest, but Weston shushes me. "I know. I was an idiot. Because when I walked into that library and saw you, my whole world came undone. You probably don't remember, but you swung your feet down onto the carpet and sat up straight and looked at me. And I'd worn my collar open that day. I'd made sure to, because I wanted you to know, right away. I wanted you to look at my Mark and see how dangerous I was and hate me the same way I hated you. Only it didn't happen like that. You looked at my triquetra, and then at my face, and you...*smiled*. This big, open thing. And..." Feeling chokes his voice. "Fortuna's curses, no one had ever done that before. Smiled at me like that. It was as if you were glad to see me. Like you'd been *waiting*, only nobody had ever waited for me, not with joy. Not with welcome. I didn't even know what that felt like until you smiled and some side of myself I'd never even touched before just...burst into existence. And that was it. I was yours. I fell in love with you in less time than it took you to blink. Even though I knew from that first moment that I could never have you."

A fresh volley of tears pricks at my eyes, even though I've cried them all out. The smile I gave him, I do remember, because I *had* been waiting. I just hadn't known it until I laid eyes on him and a jolt of recognition ran through every cell. I'd glimpsed my future in the starkly beautiful lines of that face, and even his Mark had made perfect sense to me. Because of course Fortuna would send me someone who would grant my deepest, most private wish. It would be just my luck.

Only later had I realized it wouldn't be that easy.

"The point is," he says, "I would've done anything for you right then, and it's still true now. And...I'm sorry. I'm so sorry I didn't get to you sooner. I'm sorry I didn't stop you from getting taken in the first place."

Air carves deep into my lungs. I want to tell him none of this is his fault, but I know he won't believe me, and I don't have it in me to argue right now. So I just stare up, waiting for whatever comes next.

"He'll come after you again, won't he?" he says quietly.

"Alverton?"

"Yes. No matter where I take you."

A despairing sound rises in my chest, but I shove it back down. "Yes. He had a Charm. A man he hired to find me. Someone whose luck outmatches mine. It might take a day or two, but he'll track me down again."

His jaw hardens. "Then I'll marry you. Right now. Tonight. Alverton'll have no choice but to give up his claim."

I grimace. "He won't, though. He said he'd come for me regardless. That I was bought and paid for. Because it's my Mark he wants, really. Not a wife."

Weston goes quiet, his eyes slicing shut, his whole body

quivering with some repressed emotion. When he looks at me again, he's calculating. I can sense his accountant's mind juggling probabilities, slotting them into place, coming up with some answer only he can see.

"Then I'm taking you home," he says.

"What? To Pine's End? Brendan will only—"

"No." The word is final. Steel-cut. "Home. Our home. The cabin."

Wonder wakens somewhere inside me. *Our home.* "But the duke."

"It's all right. It's going to be all right. I'll *make* it all right."

I don't dare ask what he means. I just breathe, strength seeping into me as the water in my belly finds its way into my desiccated limbs. "Okay," I whisper.

In another moment, he's gathering me up. I tuck my head against his shirtfront, breathing him in as he carries me back to the horse, which stands tall and patient in the moonlight.

Goddess, Weston smells like everything I thought I'd lost. Amber and warmth and...*safety.*

Without a word, he helps me up into the saddle. This time, I actually manage to swing my leg over, and then he's behind me, his thighs bracketing mine as he wheels the horse around. His arm settles around my waist, pulling me against his layers of fabric.

When we reach the road again, Weston turns north. Pines sprawl in every direction, but even in the starlight, I recognize a few of the landmarks we passed the day he stole the duke's carriage.

Three boulders, heaped together in a mimicry of a sleeping ogre. A tree, split down the middle by some long-ago lightning crack.

Two bushes that look like foraging chickens.

Weston guides the horse between them. On the other side, a dirt track awaits, which leads us to the same clearing he stopped the carriage in.

A light appears through the trees, beckoning.

As we draw nearer, Weston crushes me close, squeezing the breath from my body. Or maybe that's just my own anticipation, because something is about to happen. I can feel it looming.

Once that door closes behind us, everything will change.

And I don't ever want to go back, once it does.

Chapter Twenty

I nside the cabin, Weston sets gloved hands on my hips and steers me toward the fireplace. After my foray into the pool, we're both cold and damp, and while he kneels to spark a fire, I yank at the hateful wedding dress. The moment the thing dries, I'm going to burn it, just like I did the last one.

By the time Weston gets a blaze going, the gown lies in a heap on the floor. I hesitate with my chemise, my fingers tangled in the hem, but something about being back here brings Helena's words to bear.

Bold as brass.

I'm not bold in the slightest. Even less so now than before. But I tug the chemise over my head anyway, because faking it is probably better than nothing. It's also all I have at the moment.

That done, I stand there in my bra and underwear, waiting for Weston to turn around.

I'm just...waiting. Waiting and waiting and waiting. I think I've spent my whole life doing nothing else.

Goddess, please let all this waiting be at an end.

When he finishes with the fire and rises to face me, he startles. His gaze rakes over my bared body, his eyes darkening to russet gold. "Birdie? What're you doing?"

An eternity stretches between us, so heavy with longing it threatens to drag me into the floor. I know I made him a vow, and yet I can't help but ask this question, one last time.

I'm only saved by the fact that I'm not saying the words.

"Please," I say.

"I don't... I can't..." He scrubs a hand through his hair and blows out a breath, conflict warring in his face. "I can't take anything you're not ready to give. Not after what you've just been through."

A fresh sob wedges sideways in my chest. I want him *because* of what I've just been through, not in spite of it. Because the duke stole something from me, inside that room. Alverton robbed me of some vital piece of myself when he hauled me in front of a mirror, kicked me down into a kneel, and forced me to confront my own frailty. When he proved how brittle I am, how easy to break.

Weston can't give those pieces of me back. I know that. But I need to believe he still wants me. That he can look at me without seeing something Alverton smashed beyond repair.

"I need," I say.

A shiver runs through him. "What, Birdie? What do you need? Name it."

I shift my weight. "Just...you."

Naked yearning slices across his features. He steps closer, and I tip my head back. Fortuna, I'm so in love with this man. I'm in love with the fact that he came for me, that he didn't give up even though I did. I love that he walled these rooms off without meaning to, that he carved a hairbrush for me and filled the coldbox with milk. I love that my first smile for him affected him so deeply. I love his stupidly beautiful face. I love every punch he's ever thrown, and how his hair slides over his forehead when he peers down at me like this. How I only get this view of him up close.

"You're sure?" His voice drops to little more than husk and smoke. "Absolutely, one hundred percent certain?"

"Yes. Take me. Anything you want. All of it."

He makes a sound, broken and yet full of want. The inches between us crackle and pop, each one a drop of oil in a sizzling pan.

"I hope you realize," he finally says, "that if you'd died, I would have, too. I wouldn't have had a reason, anymore."

"A reason?" I murmur. "For what?"

"Anything."

Emotion seals my throat, rendering me wordless. I reach for his face, then halt my palm an inch from his cheek. His skin tugs at mine like a magnet, but I resist.

His choice. It has to be his choice.

Something ancient slides into his eyes. An inevitability. "Ten seconds, Birdie."

I blink. My hand drops. "What?"

"That's how long you have to change your mind." His gloved fingers flex at his sides. "Because I almost lost you. And it was *because* of your Mark, not in spite of it. Now ten seconds is all I have left. Ten more seconds of resisting you."

My heart lurches, straining against my ribs. "What happens after ten seconds?"

He glances behind me. "Then I lay you out on that bed, and when you get out of it again, you won't be a Charm. So think about it. Be absolutely sure."

All the room's air evaporates, leaving me gasping and dizzy. I sway on my feet. I don't need to think about anything.

"One," he says.

A whimper warms my throat. My whole body begins to buzz. I can't believe he's finally going to give me this gift. These *two* gifts. The only two things I've ever wanted, in one fell stroke.

"Two." Weston pulls his left glove off, finger by finger, then does the same with the right. He peers down at the pair as if memorizing it, then tosses the gloves into the fire.

I follow the movement, my eyes wide. "Did you just—"

"Three."

When I glance back, he's tugging his shirt free of his waistband. He works it up over his head and casts it away somewhere. I don't hear it land, lost as I am in the play of firelight across his chest. The striated muscles of his shoulders flex and bunch.

"Four," Weston says, growing hoarser by the moment.

My heartbeat skips. He kicks off his boots. In the fireplace, the gloves combust, throwing a flare of heat that warms my side.

"Five." He works at his pants until the buttons pop loose, then shoves them down. He shucks his underwear, too—all of it gone, in one clean motion. He steps free and kicks them away. "Six."

I look down. Then my eyes get stuck, because he's already ready. He *wants* me—even like this, even broken—and I want him more than I've ever wanted anything, and I can't believe this is actually happening. Alverton and his horrid little room fade from my mind.

"Seven."

I meet those familiar whiskey eyes. The scene crystallizes, etching itself on my mind.

This, right here, right now, is the defining moment of my existence. This man. Each counted second outweighs an hour spent in parched misery.

And, for a moment, I feel immeasurably lucky. Blessed by the thousand tiny collisions of fate that have delivered me to this place.

"Eight." Weston is trembling now, his wealth of power all held in check. "Nine."

"I love you," I say.

He falters. "Ten," he finishes, his voice raw.

I wait. My heart is a bird, poised to fly. When long seconds pass and Weston still doesn't move, I tilt my face up. My heartbeat catches fire. "Ruin me," I beg. "Save me."

His hesitation comes apart. He steps in, takes my face in his hands, and crushes his mouth to mine.

My eyes close. My entire body exhales, my soul softening at the sheer rightness of this. Weston's tongue probes at the seam of my lips, and I open to him like a flower. Nectar-sweet relief cascades through me.

I twine my arms around his neck. Goddess, we were always meant to do this, to be this to one another. We've been heading toward this moment since the day we first locked eyes in my library. Which means maybe, just maybe, Fortuna Marked us to bring us together, not drive us apart.

Maybe we were always meant to save one another.

Weston's hands dive into my hair, kneading my scalp, making the ends of my tresses tickle the small of my back. I pull him closer. His kiss is effervescent, like a mouthful of sparkling wine, sweetened with honey.

It's our magic, maybe, equalizing. Or maybe it's just him, this person who's saved me a thousand times over. He tastes like ambrosia. Like hope and divinity.

Then he's gathering me into his embrace and lifting me. I wrap my legs around his waist as he carries me to the bed, where he lays me out like he promised. His weight settles atop me, more binding than an oath. Because I feel it, already. The crackling hum as our opposing forces meet.

The kiss turns fierce, Weston's tongue exploring my mouth with mounting urgency. He pants hungry sounds against my lips as his hands trail fire down my sides. I scrabble at him, trying to get closer, and his fingers settle at my hips, digging in almost desperately.

When he tugs at my underwear, I lift my hips, pulling one leg through, then the other. He tosses the scrap of silk away. His lips trail down the side of my throat, his breathing ragged against my racing pulse. He unfastens my bra and throws that, too.

My whole body comes alive, lighting up like a firework. "Lick my Mark."

He obeys, leaving behind a tremor that's both hot and cold, an impossible sensation only he can elicit. I arch, needing to be against him, to be part of him. I need more. I need everything.

He pulls back just enough to gaze down into my face. "I want to be inside you when it happens," he rasps. "I want every part of you to be mine when I take your luck."

"Yes," I whimper. The buzz of our pressed-together bodies builds, cresting into an ache in my teeth. One that's only over-shadowed by the ache between my legs. "Yes, yes, yes."

"Do you need more time? More—"

"No. I want you *now*."

Weston groans, a sound of surrender and need, and his mouth fuses with mine again. The passing seconds melt to a sticky swirl. There's the brush of his calluses, the wet heat of his mouth, the solid weight of him between my thighs. And, deep within, the frantic vibration of my luck finding its opposite—its equal—and yielding to it.

He shifts his weight, notching his hips against mine, all barriers between us gone. As if to be sure, he reaches down and brushes a touch along my core.

An exquisite shiver rockets through me. We both break the kiss to look. His fingers come away slick and shining.

The buzz inside me pitches higher.

"Hurry," I whisper, so overburdened with feeling I can barely hear myself think, much less speak.

He releases a shuddery breath and looks at me, his expression stark and vulnerable in the firelight. I drop a quick glance to his Mark. It's still there, but it won't be for much longer. The internal hum crescendos to a whine, and when I raise my eyes again, I know I've looked at his triquetra for the last time.

"Now," I say.

"We'll go slow next time."

"Next time," I agree. And I want to die of joy, knowing there will be a next time.

He reaches down to set himself against my entrance. He takes my face in his hands. Then he's pushing, stretching, filling me. Saving me. Freeing me. I cry out at the sensation, my fingernails biting into his shoulders. Those whiskey eyes hold me in place, and a bolt of tenderness spears me, so pure it nearly tears a hole in my chest.

A hoarse sound wrenches from his throat. He chases it up with a curse. "Incredible. You feel incredible."

I tilt my hips until I have all of him. "*You* do. Feel... Oh... My goddess."

He eases back, then in again, driving a ripple of bliss through me. My lashes flutter, but I force my eyes to stay open, because I want to witness this. All of it. Every last drop.

Another muffled groan rolls out of him. "Is this okay?"

"Yes." I frame his face with my palms. "Goddess, yes. More."

He anchors a hand to the back of my neck. He begins to move in earnest, claiming me, making me his even though I already belong to him, and I lift my hips to meet every roll of his. I exist as slices of sensation, each stacked atop the next until they threaten to topple. There's Weston's hair, brushing my forehead as he holds my eyes. His fingertips against my nape, a string of searing, glowing touchpoints. The feel of him inside me, reshaping me into the exact thing I've always hoped to be.

Luckless. His.

We ravel tight, tangling into a knot of moans and sweat-slicked skin. Sparks fly and catch inside me. I cling to him as he chases a rhythm that promises to tip me over some fast-approaching edge.

"Touch me," I gasp out. "With your fingers, too."

"Where?" The word is ragged.

I uncurl his hand from my neck and steer it downward between our bodies. He splays his palm across my belly, letting me set his thumb against the spot—that wonderful spot—that makes stars collide behind my eyes. I guide his finger back and forth. A cry slips from my lips as each pass inspires a burst of pleasure.

I let go, but he continues the movement. "This is how you like it?"

"Yes," I manage. "It's how I touch myself. At night. While I think about you."

A light gathers in his eyes, so bright it's volcanic. The sound that rumbles from his chest is nothing short of feral.

"What else?" he demands. "What else do you think about me doing to you?"

"This." I widen my legs, granting him deeper access, and he takes it. He surges into me and simultaneously works me with his thumb, assaulting me with a double dose of pleasure I can barely withstand.

"Always, exactly this," I bite out.

"I've dreamed of it, too," he rasps. "But this is so much better."

It is. It's consuming. But I can't tell him that, because words have abandoned me. I'm spinning into myself, falling down, down, down, into a crashing river of sensation. Weston drives me deeper with every flex of his body, every press of his thumb. My spine bows up off the mattress.

Light collects behind my eyes, a rising force. And then he's slingshotting me out into the abyss. Ecstasy takes me, spiraling outward to the tips of my fingers and toes. I shatter beneath him, crying out his name.

A moment later, he follows. His hips stutter against mine as he finds his release. "Bria," he gasps, the syllables reverent.

Words pour from my mouth. I can't even say which ones. Weston's name again, maybe, tangled with curses. A promise to love him ten more years, and the ten after that. I cling to him, riding out the waves.

He buries his face in the side of my neck and, when the intensity ebbs, slowly goes lax. Tension bleeds out of me, too, leaving me syrupy and melted. The clang of my pulse eases to a hum.

He eventually raises his head. His mouth finds mine, the kiss an outpouring of emotion—relief, awe, a devotion so deep it steals the breath from my lungs.

I kiss him back with abandon. A tear slips from the corner of my eye.

"Thank you," I say into his mouth. Then I say it again, because those words are too small to hold the immensity of my gratitude. "Thank you, thank you, thank you."

"Shh," he says, sealing my lips shut with a kiss. "I'm the one who should be saying that to you."

He pulls back enough for me to bring him into focus. The space between his clavicles is bare. Perfect. A blank canvas.

My lungs squeeze. I didn't feel my magic go—or maybe I did, but the moment got lost inside all the others, and that feels right, somehow, not being able to locate the second in which my wish was granted, because another, more important miracle, was taking place.

He cups my cheek, his brows knitting. "Are you all right? Did I hurt you?"

"Not at all. Just the opposite."

He hesitates. "How do you feel?"

I give in to a contented sigh. "Perfect," I say, because there's no other possible answer when he's still inside me. "Absolutely perfect."

That seems to comfort him, because the tension in his face eases, some.

"You?" I sound dreamy and sated.

"I feel like...I should probably let you rest. After these last few days..." His voice catches, loaded with feeling.

I reach up to caress his face. The wonder of it nearly undoes me. I'm *touching* him. Like it's nothing. Like it's normal. Joy rises in me, so thick and wild it nearly stops my heart. "You'll stay with me tonight? On this side?"

"Do you want me to?"

"Of course."

He smiles, if a little reluctantly. He eases out of me and stands.

My brow wrinkles. "Wait, where're you going?"

"Not far. I'll be right back."

I blink as he moves toward the door, then give up and slump into the pillows. Exhaustion drags at me, crowding to fill the spaces his absence leaves behind. The door opens and shuts. My eyes flutter.

I even sleep for a moment, I think. Then Weston is back, setting something down on the pinewood stand beside the bed. I open my eyes.

Tenderness catches in my throat. A glass of milk.

He helps me into a sit. I drink. And drink, and Fortuna, simple milk has never nourished a person more. It slides down my still-raw throat like a balm. Even my belly relaxes, gifted, at last, with something to digest.

"Thank you," I tell him again.

He flashes a fleeting smile. "Do you need anything else?"

"Just you."

He studies me, and I don't think I'm imagining the beat of

hesitation, even though it's done. It's over. Nothing separates us any longer.

I open my mouth to ask what's wrong, but he settles beside me, gathering me close, and the question slips out of my head. I'm so tired. I tuck my face beneath his chin, marveling that we can finally hold each other. No fabric, no barriers, no magic keeping us apart. Just Weston and me, as we always should have been.

I take a moment to savor the steady rhythm of his heartbeat against my cheek, the weight of his arm around my waist. For so long, I've dreamed that we would share a bed like this. That I would drift off enfolded in his warmth, lulled by the gentle rise and fall of his chest.

"Sleep," he murmurs, his lips brushing my hair. "You're safe."

With those words wrapped around my heart, I let my eyes drift closed.

I *do* need rest, I know. Because tomorrow, or the next day, Ramses and the duke will come for me.

Only this time, they won't find what they're looking for.

Chapter Twenty-One

When I wake, I reach for Weston.

My arm encounters a gulf of cold, empty sheets. I sit up, my heartbeat knotted with panic. Where is he? He wouldn't have left, would he? What if Alverton came and took him? What if—

A glance across the room soothes the discordant chaos within me. Weston stands before the pump-handled sink, his hands braced on the counter, the musculature of his back standing at attention. He's stark naked. My eyes slide down over his backside, lingering on the divots at the base of his spine. "What're you doing?"

He doesn't answer. He doesn't even move. It's like he hasn't heard me at all.

A frown drags at my mouth. "Weston?"

Nothing.

I slide from bed and pad toward him, the chilled floorboards sucking warmth from my soles. When I get close, I see he's staring in the mirror, his eyes fixed low on the glass. As if—

Understanding flashes. He's looking at his Mark. Or lack thereof.

I lay a hand on his arm. He jumps at the touch, his gaze swinging to mine.

His eyes are bright and feverish. "My triquetra. It's..."

I wait, but he doesn't continue. "Gone," I offer gently. "You're rid of it."

His attention falls to my throat. He flinches at what he finds there. "Yours, too. I... Oh, goddess, Birdie, what did I do to you?"

I reach up to brush a few golden strands back. His eyes are wild. Flame-bitten and frantic.

"You gave me everything I've ever wanted," I say. "You freed me."

He swallows, the sound of it harsh in the cold room.

I hesitate. I should've known he might react like this. That he might regret, once daylight had driven away yesterday's mountain of horrors. I should've realized he'd struggle with losing the curse he believed he deserved, even if it's a blessing for both of us.

"It's okay." I pull at him, and he doesn't resist. He curls into me, his face landing against my chest, his back rising and falling with jerky movements. And... Fortuna, is he crying?

My heart splinters apart. I fist my hands in his hair, clutching him close.

"I'm sorry," he says against my skin. "I'm so sorry."

"I'm not." I imbue the words with as much force as they can hold. "Not for a second. Everything that happened last night was my choice. I don't regret any of it. I have nothing but gratitude for what you did."

Air staggers into his chest, and suddenly he's kissing me,

the press of his mouth frenzied against mine. His cheeks are wet, his lips salted.

I can't tell whether he means to take from me or give, but whatever he needs, I'll provide it. He can have anything. I offer it freely.

"Tell me you still love me," he chokes out. "Even after what I've done."

"I love you. *More* than I did yesterday, not less."

He makes a sound that might be acceptance or denial, I can't tell, but whatever it is, it's laced in pain, and when he catches me up and hoists me onto the counter, I splay my legs apart. I don't hesitate. Not for a second.

Within moments, he's inside me, and while I know that someday we'll go slow, it isn't today, because he needs something from me and I need to give it to him and I'll do anything, anything to save him from this misplaced guilt.

He takes me hard. Unrelenting. And yet it lasts, like he's asking me a question and listening to my answer, over and over again, never quite believing the truth of what my body is confessing. I hold him the whole time. My fists ravel in his hair, keeping his forehead anchored to mine.

I offer him everything. I keep my eyes open and my heart bared. I don't look away and neither does he, even when he surges deep and stays there, his every tendon straining as he clutches me close. I take in the short, choppy jumps of his breathing, the glistening dilation of his pupils as he comes apart.

He does it all in silence, as if he doesn't dare impose on the quiet. As if he doesn't think he deserves to. Part of me shears away, sliced through by the knowledge that, even curseless, he still believes himself unworthy.

His head finally falls against my shoulder, then lolls. His muscles unstitch themselves, one by one.

I wrap my arms tighter and hook my ankles behind his thighs. I prop my chin on his shoulder and close my eyes and just hold him.

Right up until the moment someone flings open the door. The wood cracks against the frame. A blur of color and finery storms into the room.

I shriek. Weston's whole body jerks to attention. He instinctively moves to cover me, his hands coming up to shield my breasts. When he turns his head, a snarl has already screwed itself into place.

I cower, unable to face the duke again so soon, only...

Horror-struck green eyes regard me from over Weston's shoulder. Eyes that look an awful lot like mine.

"Brendan?" I yelp. Dismay opens a pit inside me. "What're you doing here?"

My brother takes in our state of affairs and flings up a hand, shielding his eyes. He angles his whole body away. "Fortuna," he sputters. "What're *you* doing? You're... You're... Curses, can you put some clothes on? What the hell did I just walk in on?"

"Something private," Weston growls. "So I suggest you walk right back out."

Brendan makes a swatting motion in our direction and ducks away, practically diving through the door in his haste to retreat. I start to unwind myself from Weston, but he doesn't let me. He picks me up from the counter and carries me to the bed as if it costs him nothing.

He sets me down and digs in my trunk for a dress, which he hands over. While I tug the thing on, he searches for our fallen clothes and steps into his breeches. That done, he makes for the door.

"Stay here," he says.

I don't, of course. The second I'm decent, I rush out after him. Brendan waits in the middle of the clearing, red-cheeked and fuming. Weston barrels toward him, and...

Oh.

I know what's going to happen well before it does, because I've seen that same stride in the ring. Seen him prowl like that, every step bursting with intent.

Sure enough, Weston reaches my brother, cocks back a fist, and drives it straight into Brendan's face.

My brother careens backward, landing on his back in the grass. Weston spits and makes a noise that's part animal, then stands there, his back heaving, his fists clenched at his sides.

"You traitor." It's a deadly shout that's also somehow half-whisper. "You miserable asshole. You selfish fuck."

"Me?" Brendan's indignant holler startles a raven from a nearby tree. "*Me*, selfish? When you're the one who just had your hands on my sister? How does that make sense? And what the hell did you just hit me for?"

"For promising Bria to a man who *tortured* her," Weston spits. "For the fact that she almost died in Alverton's custody. And for what? So you could buy yourself another fucking waistcoat?"

Brendan sits up, blinking hard. He drags the back of a hand across his mouth, seemingly surprised when it comes away coated in red. "I... What?"

"He almost killed her!" Weston shouts with unallayed fury. "He locked her in a room without a drop of water! For days!"

My brother's eyes pop wide. His gaze seeks mine as if magnetized. And when his stare locks into place, I see it.

The moment he realizes my throat is bare.

All the color drains from his cheeks. His attention jumps to Weston, plainly searching for confirmation. Which he finds, of course.

He chokes on his own air supply. "What the... What'd you do? What the hell did you do to Bria?"

Exactly what I asked him to, I want to shout, only I can't get the words out, because Weston rears back from Brendan's vitriol as if stabbed.

It's the worst thing my brother could have said. The one thing guaranteed to wound.

I force my frozen tongue to cooperate. "Brendan, no. It's not like that. I asked him to—"

My words die as movement at the treeline catches my eye. A man on horseback stands at the edge of the clearing, his features obscured by the brim of his hat. But even at this distance, a chill of recognition skitters down my spine. My bare toes curl into the grass.

Not possible.

Yet even as denial surges up my throat, the man coaxes his mount forward. Light hits his face. Air abandons my lungs as readily as if someone punched me in the stomach.

"Dad?" I say.

Chapter Twenty-Two

My father's face settles into stern lines as he takes in the scene—Weston with his fists clenched, Brendan with blood dripping from his chin, me in my simple dress, my triquetra stripped away.

And I catch it, even from twenty feet away. A towering disappointment rising in my father's eyes. A whole, looming wall of it, threatening to collapse and bury me beneath the rubble.

He just witnessed this entire exchange.

"What's he doing here?" I say to Brendan—not accusing, just...flabbergasted. Beyond confused. Blank.

"What do you mean? He's been back for weeks." My brother spits red, then scrambles gracelessly to his feet. "Him and Mom both. They came home when you went missing. Of course they did."

He says it like it's obvious, and yet...it isn't. Not to me. I never once considered that my father might show up here. I barely suspected my brother would.

"We've been looking for this place, all this time," Brendan

continues. "I mean, we *thought* Weston might be the one who'd taken you. We hoped. But..." His mouth curls into a sneer as he surveys his best friend. "We thought he'd watch over you. Not *defile* you."

Weston takes another jerky step backward, his shoulders curving as if to ward off Brendan's accusation.

"Stop!" I screech. "Don't you say another word to him, unless it's to thank him. He didn't defile me, he saved me. And he only took my Mark because I asked him to. It was my choice."

Brendan's eyes flash. "His, too. Don't pretend he didn't know what he was doing. What he was stealing from you."

Weston's fists go slack at his sides. All the fight leaves him.

For a moment, no one moves. In the silence, my father slips from his saddle and makes his way over to me.

I shrink back from every oncoming step. I always imagined my parents' homecoming as a happy affair—they'd gone off to tour the continent, leaving Brendan with one objective: find me a suitable husband before they came home.

Now he's failed them. So have I, but by an order of magnitude more.

When my father reaches me, he crushes me in a hug. Shock holds me motionless for a moment before I raise my arms. But he's already thrusting me away again, gripping me by the shoulders, pointing a grief-stricken look at the space between my collarbones. "You're okay," he says. "But not whole."

My mouth twists. I tug against his grip.

He holds me in place without much effort. "The Null boy did this to you?"

"No," I insist. "I mean, yes, technically, but only because I asked him to."

Weston tips his face to the sky, his hands pressed to his eyes as if he can't bear to look at any of us. My blood screams. I can *feel* him slipping away from me. I can see it happening.

"We're taking you home," my father says.

"No, I—"

"He desecrated you." My father raises his voice, the words clearly intended for Weston, even though he's looking at me. "We allowed this Null into our home. We trusted him, and he disrespected our family."

"No!" I swat at him until he releases my shoulders. "I love him. I'm going to marry him. He saved my life. I'd be dead right now if not for him, or at least married to Alverton, and—"

"And you'd have your Mark!" my father cuts in. "You'd still be you!"

I recoil, my blood stilling inside my veins. "I *am* still me," I whisper.

But my father's words cut deep, down to some secret, boarded-up place, where I've stored up all the memories, the expectations, the endless tea parties my mother used to throw. She would give me a sweet before her friends arrived and tell me to interrupt her later. When I inevitably did, she'd hoist me onto her knee, putting my Mark at eye level, and wait for some happy little accident to occur. Minnie might arrive with more tea bags just as the last was lifted from the pot, or a curl would fall from my mother's bun in a single, stylish corkscrew, and she'd laugh and detail the many delights of having a Charm in the house.

Now I've taken that pride of hers and stabbed it dead. I'll never again be the person she preened over.

My hand cinches around the base of my throat, trying to ease the sudden ache there.

"Get on the horse," my father says.

I look to Weston. He's on his knees in the grass now, his spine curled, his body folded, his beautiful strength nowhere to be found.

Brendan spits at him and wipes at his bloodied nose again. "Were you ever really my friend? Or was this about you the whole time? About using Bria to break your curse?"

Weston doesn't react, but the barb lands. I can't say how I know, except that his stillness is horrible, as if he's been shot full of arrows and is just waiting to die.

"I'm sorry," he mumbles.

"Fuck you," Brendan replies.

I want to scream. I want to break something.

"Get on the horse, Bria," my father says. "We're taking you home."

I rage in silence, waiting for Weston to protest, or for me to, or for Fortuna to sweep in and arrange some way to keep me here.

Only she doesn't. Of course not. She never will again. I made sure of that.

"Get. On. The horse." My father's tone brooks no argument.

I flinch at the bite in his tone. Weston refuses to look at me.

And so, in the end, I do what I've always done.

I do as I'm told.

Chapter Twenty-Three

At home, my mother takes one look at me and bursts into tears.

"My sweet girl." She faces me in the middle of the parlor, her lace-gloved hands flitting over my skin as if testing its integrity. "Oh, my girl, no, no, no, what did he do to you?"

I answer without thinking. "Alverton, you mean?"

"No, that Null boy. He...touched you, didn't he? Oh, goddess. He forced you? Don't tell me he forced you. What is this world coming to, when Nulls are allowed to go around assaulting Charms for their—"

"Mom."

She blinks. Tears course down her cheeks.

"What're you even talking about? You know Weston. You've known him for ten years. Of course he didn't hurt me."

Her eyes fall to my collarbones, then skew away just as quickly, like she can't bear to look. She presses a hand over her mouth and sobs.

My father stands in the corner, his arms crossed, his

expression hard. "He might not have hurt you, but he took from you, nonetheless. He took from all of us. This whole family."

A boulder lands in my throat, a burning ball of outrage. I have to squeeze my next words past it. "That's ridiculous. Weston *saved* me. He came and got me when the duke locked me up. When Alverton starved me. And afterward, he only unMarked me because I begged him to. He didn't *force* anything."

Brendan hunches in an armchair, studying his clasped fists, but at my words, he raises his head. He hasn't cleaned himself up. Dried blood crusts his chin and shirtfront. "What do you mean? About Alverton? I thought Weston was just saying that."

"No. He was telling the truth."

"The duke...hurt you?"

I clench my teeth. "He did more than that. He nearly killed me. He locked me in a room without any food or water for almost three days. By the time Weston got to me, I couldn't stand. I could barely even talk."

Horror dawns in Brendan's eyes. My mother wails, but we both ignore her.

"I don't understand." My father frowns. "Why would Alverton offer such an enormous sum for you, then try to kill you?"

A shudder eddies through me. "Because. He thought he could force me to be the meek little wife he wanted. He thought he could break me."

And he was absolutely right, I don't add.

"But..." Brendan searches for words. "How could he have managed that? What about Fortuna? Your Mark?"

"It didn't matter. The duke had a man who was just as lucky as I was. Luckier, even. Another Charm. And the Charm wanted me locked up, so it happened."

My brother swallows. He looks like he's choking on his own tongue. "I can't... You're saying I promised you to a man who tortured you? *I* did that?"

I can see it. He wants me to say no. To take it all back. His eyes beg me to. But I don't have that much grace. "Yes. You did."

He plunges both hands through his hair, leaving it an unprecedented mess, then shoots out of the chair and strides from the room without another word.

"Maybe we could tattoo it back on," my mother says.

My head snaps around. "What?"

"Your Mark. We could tattoo it back on. No one would know the difference."

Some slimy, dark thing drops into my guts. "Are you kidding me? Did you hear a word I just said? About Alverton?"

But she's crying again, her makeup running in smears down her cheeks, her response garbled by hiccups. "There's a tattoo artist in Hay—"

"Mom!" I stamp my foot. "No. Just stop. You're being horrible. I'm not getting a tattoo, and this is why I hated being a Charm. It was exactly this, right here."

Her sobs cut off abruptly, replaced by a shocked stare. If she had pearls, she'd probably be clutching them, but as it stands, diamonds and emeralds drip from her throat, so she only presses a hand to her chest. "What?" she whispers.

"You heard me." I dart a glance at my father, including him

in my confession. "I never wanted my Mark. I hated it. I'm glad it's gone. I'm glad that..."

A sound from outside makes me trail off. I cock an ear. Hoofbeats sound in the distance—faint, at first, then louder.

Someone is cantering up the driveway.

My soul lightens. Weston. It has to be. He's recovered from Brendan's horrible insults and followed me here. He's come for me again, because he always will.

Elation gifts me with wings. I arrow toward the window, but when I push the curtain aside—

I freeze, terror harpooning me in the chest. I blink, trying to wish the scene away, but nothing changes. "No. *No.*"

It's Alverton. The duke's face is stern, his brow low. Ramses rides at his side. They're already halfway up the driveway. They'll be here in less than a minute. Right on my doorstep.

I scramble back, overturning a side table in the process. A vase careens to the floor and smashes, spraying chips of porcelain, but the sound barely reaches me. I'm a white-hot rain of fear. I'm back in that room. I'm dissolving into terror and no one is here to save me and—

"Go upstairs," my father says. "Now. I'll deal with this."

I don't stop to question him. I lift my skirts and race up the stairs, careening around the corner and racing down the hall to my room. I slam the door with full-body force and dive into my closet, then pull those doors closed, too. I press myself into the furthest, darkest corner, where I hug my knees and try not to hyperventilate.

It doesn't work. Oxygen pours into me, so much that my head spins and my toes tingle, as if I've singed them against the blazing edges of my dread.

Long minutes pass. Time is a razor, slicing and slicing at me.

Shouting erupts downstairs. I can hear it through the floor, though I can't catch the words. I'm shaking. Downstairs, something breaks. A door slams. A heavy tread mounts the stairs, and I cower deeper into the closet. I can't go back. I can't. I'll die. I'll—

The doors open. It's Brendan, outlined by the sunlight streaming through my bedroom windows. Without a word, he pushes his way past the hanging gowns and furs, then settles beside me with his back against the wall. He doesn't look at me.

"He's gone," he says. "You're safe."

I hug my knees tighter, waiting for my fear to abate. For my body to stop trembling. But it doesn't. For some reason, those words don't sound nearly as convincing coming from my brother as they did from Weston.

Brendan sighs and lets his head fall back against the wall. "Alverton really did all that? Nearly killed you?"

I blink, wondering if this is a trick. But I can't see how, so I say, "He did." The words are like broken glass being dragged up my throat.

Brendan winces. "I'm sorry. Fortuna's curses, I'm so sorry. I thought I was doing right by you. I thought your luck would take care of you."

My hold on my knees loosens a degree. That's...not what I expected him to say.

"Alverton won't come back." Brendan sounds distant, almost like he's talking to himself. "He lost interest the moment Dad told him your Mark was gone. He's furious, and he's demanding to have his money returned, *with* interest, but he won't come back."

I press a hand to my chest, willing my heart to settle. "Did Dad—"

"Punched him. Not as hard as Weston would have. But he did it. He tried to punch that creepy Charm, too, but he tripped. No surprise there, I guess."

I have no response for that.

Brendan sighs, his gaze fixed on some point in the distance, far beyond the closet, beyond even my room. "They'll never let you marry Weston, Bria. You realize that, don't you? They probably wouldn't have anyway, but now that you're unMarked... As far as they're concerned, he's ruined you."

I gulp down the raw thing clawing to life in my chest. "I know."

But I don't care what they think. I'll wait for Weston as long as I have to. When he comes, we'll steal away together. This time, we'll go to the courthouse before anyone can stop us.

Brendan turns his head to look at me. Finally. "Why didn't you ever tell me? What he was to you?"

I consider. At last, the furor inside me relaxes its grip. "I did. I tried. But you never listened. You were so caught up in what you wanted that what I wanted was just an inconvenience."

He grimaces. "I've been a bad brother, haven't I?"

"You...haven't been the best."

He nods in concession and resumes his mile-long stare.

"Come on," he finally says, after a minute of silence. "Let's get you into the bath. I'll go find Minnie. Tell her to get you cleaned up and get you fed. Then we can all go back to normal."

I chuff a humorless laugh. "Is that what I am now? Normal?"

My brother rubs at his eyes. "I don't know. I honestly don't. I guess that's kind of up to you, isn't it?"

Chapter Twenty-Four

Weston doesn't come for me that day. Or the next.

My mother fusses over me relentlessly. So does Minnie. Even my father treats me with kid gloves, as if I might shatter at the slightest provocation.

The worst part is, he's not wrong. I can no longer stand to have my bedroom door closed at night, and every morning, I drink three glasses of water, first thing, *just in case*. Then, when I sleep again, my dreams swerve into nightmare territory. I'm back in that locked room, only the walls are compressing, making a slow inward march that will end with me breaking to bits. Sometimes, Ramses appears and snags me by the wrist, his poisonous magic searing my skin.

More than once, I wake up screaming.

Two weeks slip by that way. Two weeks during which Weston doesn't come.

Brendan haunts the hallways, quieter than usual. When I catch him looking at me, there's something in his face I don't recognize. I try to ask whether he's seen his best friend, but he only says Weston hasn't returned to Pine's End, that no one has heard from him in weeks. That the cotton mill even hired a new accountant and everything.

My heart sinks. I can't imagine what's taking Weston so long. Then again, my brother dealt him a nearly fatal blow out at the cabin, and he probably needs time to recover. To remember that he means everything to me. That I'll want him until I'm dead.

Maybe after that, too.

I spend my days at the second-floor window, studying the empty drive. A few times, I try to take my horse out for a ride —a very long one that ends in a pine-ringed clearing ten miles from here—but my mother forbids it. I'm still recovering, she says. Still settling into my new self, healing from what the duke did to me.

She isn't wrong, either.

Because while I thought I would feel like some new person after losing my Mark, I don't. I may have shed my luck, but it turns out being deprived of your shield doesn't magically make you a more capable fighter. It just renders you defenseless.

Because even now, restored to comfort and safety, part of me remains in Alverton's room, huddled and shaking in the dark.

The days bleed together. I take refuge in books, losing myself in tales where evil is vanquished and love conquers all. The heroines are always brave, resourceful, unbreakable— everything I wish I could be. But that's the magic of books, I guess. They're not real.

Incessantly, I think of Weston. His absence is a wound that gapes wider by the day, and I increasingly keep vigil at the window, searching for a glimpse of gold—gold hair, gold eyes, golden skin. Any day now, he'll come for me.

But he doesn't. And eventually, my hope begins to starve.

What if he doesn't want me anymore? What if he's off enjoying some curseless, Markless new life, without the question of what he did for me weighing him down?

The possibility makes me feel like someone is sharpening steely knives against the underside of my ribs. I cycle between desperation and despair.

Then, three weeks and two days after I return home, I'm standing before my mirror, brushing my hair—I've stopped letting Minnie do it—when my mother slips into my room. She wears a smile so wide it nearly blinds me.

"Bria." Her voice brims with barely restrained excitement. "Come downstairs, won't you? There's someone here we'd like you to speak with. A visitor."

My heart stutters to a stop. "A visitor? What? Who is it?"

She claps her hands together. "A suitor. He's made an offer for you. A *generous* one. Even though you've lost your Mark. Isn't that wonderful?"

The silver hairbrush falls from my grip. I don't bother to look at where it falls. Every time I use the stupid thing, I only long for one made from wood. One that has my initials singed into the back.

Now, at long last, I won't have to wish anymore, because Weston is downstairs. This must be what the delay was about —him finding a way to approach my parents with the one thing that would sway their minds.

Money.

I take off running. I burst into the hallway, then zip down

the stairs. My heart launches higher with every step I take toward the parlor. He's here. He's come for me.

Finally, finally, finally.

I'm going to hug him. I'm going to fling myself into his arms and kiss him senseless, right in front of everybody.

I turn the corner, skid into the room, and—

Stop dead. Brendan and my father sit on the divan together. Across from them, rising as I enter, is the foreman from the mill. Calder. The one who let me use the antiseptic in his office.

"Miss Bria," he says with a formal bow.

I stand there and gape. No. This isn't right. This isn't how it's supposed to be.

He crosses the room and takes my hand. I can only stare as he presses a courteous kiss to my knuckles.

"Bria." My father gestures toward a chair. "Sit down, why don't you?"

I don't move. "What... What is this?"

Calder darts a look at me, shy and hopeful. "Well, it's a proposal. Or a reaffirmation of one, I guess I should say. I've discussed it with your father, and my offer hasn't changed. My *feelings* haven't, even if your circumstances have. I'd be just as honored to call you my wife without your Mark as with it."

I blink at him. Then scan him head to toe, certain I'm seeing him for the first time. He gives me a wobbly smile, then takes off his cap and rolls the thing in his hands, his knuckles white around the fabric.

"I could get down on one knee, if you like." He seems flustered by my silence. "Or... Well, whatever you want. Just tell me."

In the span of a heartbeat, my regard for him expands tenfold. Maybe those ninety-nine proposals *weren't* all the same.

But that doesn't mean I'm going to marry this man. I *can't*.

"Bria," my father says. "Sit. Down."

I don't. Calder flushes and starts listing all the ways he'll care for me, everything he'll strive to provide, but I can't hear him.

Because I'm standing frozen, poised on the razor's edge between my future and my past. Something new unfurls inside me, fragile and defiant. A seed of resolve, cracking open, reaching for the light.

Fortuna, I'm hiding, aren't I? Still. I'm *waiting*. I may have ridded myself of my luck, but I haven't gotten rid of my reliance, because all my life, I've waited to be saved. By Fortuna. My Mark. Weston. And it worked. Which is why I kept doing it. Over and over and over again.

But this whole time, I should have been saving myself. Or trying to, at least. Because no one is going to cede me control over my own life. Certainly not my parents. They'll only sell me to the highest bidder, like Brendan tried to.

Which means if I want control, I have to *take* it. I have to stand up, walk out of Alverton's horrible little room, and shut the door behind me. And maybe that doesn't mean I've left it broken. Maybe I've just left it changed.

Bold as brass.

"I'm sorry, Calder." The words spill out before I can stop them. "I'm touched. So very touched. Your offer means more than you know. But I can't accept."

My father makes a gruff, annoyed sound. "Bria. This is just

a formality. We've been discussing for weeks, and I've already—"

"No," I say. "No, it's my life, and I'll decide what to do with it. And I'm not marrying Calder."

Calder blinks. Once. Twice. "Is my offer unclear in some way, or—"

"No. It's not you, believe me. It's just..." I falter, groping for the proper words. "My heart belongs to someone else. It wouldn't be fair to you to pretend otherwise."

"Bria Iris Radcliffe." My father stands now, his low growl deadly with promise. "This isn't about that Null boy again, is—"

"Yes." I whirl on him. "It is. It's always been about him, and his name's Weston. And he's not a Null anymore. And he's definitely not a boy. And I don't care if you approve of him, because you don't need to. Anyway. I'm leaving now."

I turn away, only to almost run straight into Calder. "You're lovely. Really. I hope you can understand."

He regards me for a long moment. Then he nods, slowly, as if coming to some silent decision. "I wish you well, Miss Bria. Every happiness. Truly."

Goddess. He's going to make some woman incredibly lucky, someday. She just won't be me.

I step around him and aim for the door. My father leaps up from the divan, moving to intercept me, but Brendan snakes out a hand and snatches his wrist. My father tugs, but Brendan holds on tight.

I pause, bewildered. My brother can't be...helping me, can he?

"Go," Brendan says. "Quickly. I'll make sure you have enough time."

I gawk, even as wild, desperate hope sings in my chest. My father pulls and shouts, but I don't stay to witness it. I pelt from the room and through the foyer, then out the door, headed for the stables. Somewhere behind me, my mother shrieks, apparently having made it down from the second floor, but I only increase my pace.

In the stables, I snatch a cloak off a peg and saddle my yellow mare, then hop astride and race out into the chilly afternoon.

Ten miles to go.

I clear the driveway and steal a glance behind me. No one is following, at least not yet. And I'm lighter than my father. Faster.

Even if he does catch up, it'll only be after I reach the cabin, and Weston can take him in a fistfight. If that happens, I won't even intervene. I'm done trying to talk sense into my parents.

But...

My heart withers to a pitiful husk when I think of how much time has passed. Weston might not actually be at the cabin. Brendan cut him down so ruthlessly that day. What if he never recovered? What if he thinks he *did* spoil me, or disrespect me, or whatever nonsense my brother spewed in the heat of anger?

What if Weston left?

I spur my horse faster. Pines roar past while the wind slices at my cheeks.

Fear opens a void within me, one that might never be filled, because I may have let everything slip through my fingers. I might have waited too long.

Yet I keep going, because there's only one way to find out.

And because it's time, finally, to make my own luck.

Chapter Twenty-Five

By the time I locate the hollow where Weston stopped the carriage—the place where we first kissed, even if I didn't realize it at the time—my heart is a tornado in my throat.

I don't know what I'll do if the cabin is empty. Track down Helena, maybe. Ask her where her nephew might have gone. If she can't tell me, I'll try Ravenfell. And if I don't find Weston there, I'll check the next town. And the next.

I guide my horse through the hollow and into the trees, not wasting a second on walking. Branches nip at my face as the mare carries me along the path to the cabin.

Fortuna help me, I internally beg. *Let him be there, please.*

It's the last favor I'll ever ask of the goddess, I vow it.

The trees part. The clearing unfolds before me.

And my chest seizes. Because there he is, in the October sunshine, facing away, shirtless and with an axe in hand. I haul the reins hard, jerking my mare to a stop.

Then I just stare, my ability to breathe forgotten. "Beautiful" is a word that can't even touch this man. As I watch, he sets a log atop a chopping stump, then takes aim with the axe and brings the blade down, splitting the wood into halves. One skitters across the withered grass toward me. Weston chases it, his head down, the axe gripped by the haft.

When he reaches the log, he catches sight of the mare's hooves and freezes.

He looks up.

My world cranks to a halt. Those tawny eyes widen. Then Weston's brows snap low, drawing a cruel line across his features.

My pulse wobbles.

Weston straightens. Slowly. Despite the chill, he's slicked in sweat, and he is...not happy to see me.

In fact, he looks downright *angry*.

"Bria."

I flinch. This isn't how I imagined our reunion. At all. "Um. Hi."

His gaze peels away from mine, fixing on some distant point across the clearing. "If you're here to tell me about your engagement, I already know. So. You shouldn't have bothered. Congratulations, though."

The forest goes quiet, the burble of birdcall fading. I pore over his words, again and again, but they don't make any more sense the fourth time than the first. "Engagement? What're you talking about? I'm not engaged."

His eyes flick to my left hand. "Oh. Already married, then, I guess." He sniffs and resumes his study of the treeline, despite the fact that my ring finger is bare.

I shake my head, trying to clear the fog of confusion, but it does me no good. "Weston? Will you look at me? What're you *talking* about?"

His jaw hardens, taking on a mulish cast. "Your marriage. To Calder Hawthorne. You don't need to be gentle about it, or anything. I've known for a while. And I'm happy for you. Really. Calder's a good man. He was one of the only ones who would actually set foot in the ring with me. He'll be good to you. Your dad and I agree on that, at least."

Shock makes my vision fade at the edges. "My dad? When did you see my dad?"

He scowls. "When I came to see how you were doing. And to propose to you. Again. Which was...what, three times? Four? You'd think by the time I lost track, I'd have realized it wasn't going to work out for me. But you know what they say."

I don't know what they say. And I am...so lost. So I try again. "I'm not married, Weston. Or engaged. Calder Hawthorne did propose, but I turned him down."

He blinks. His gaze slides to me.

"And what do you mean, 'you know what they say?' What do they say, exactly?"

He hesitates. He runs a hand through his gilded hair, which takes the opportunity to spring every which way. "You know. That proverb you always hear."

"*What* proverb?"

Color seeps into his cheeks. "Hope springs eternal," he finally says.

A shiver coils at the base of my spine. Something about that answer feels so violently appropriate that I drop the reins entirely. "So...you're saying you came to my house? *After* the last time I saw you in this clearing? And you proposed to me, via my father?"

He squints. "Didn't he tell you?"

Wingbeats erupt inside my chest. "No. Did you honestly expect him to?"

"Well, I thought..." He looks taken aback by my father's duplicity. "I mean, I guess he didn't say, one way or the other. But he told you were already promised to Calder Hawthorne. And that you'd been struggling ever since... Since..."—he swallows hard—"Since I did what I did to you. And that you'd be better off never seeing me again. Because if I'd been the sort of man who deserved you, I never would've—"

"Stop." I wave a hand. "Just stop. You realize that's all horseshit, right? Everything you just said."

His mouth clicks shut. He peers at me, his golden stare lancing through the dark fringe of his lashes. "It's not. He was right."

"No," I say. "He was dead wrong. Because I've been *waiting* for you. All this time. And maybe I *was* struggling, a little, but only because I hadn't realized the extent of the gift you gave me. I didn't understand the losing my Mark meant that Fortuna doesn't control me anymore. That I control myself, now. That, for as much as I wished my triquetra away, the important part wasn't losing it, but learning to stand on my own. But I get it now. And I have you to thank."

He narrows his eyes, skeptical. "You shouldn't be thanking me for anything. I betrayed you. I did something awful to you. The one thing I'd always promised not to do."

I heave a sigh. "Weston... You didn't do anything *to* me, you did it *for* me. And even if I'm different now, my feelings aren't. I still love you. I still think about you every second. I still touch myself at night and pretend it's you. I think I love you even more, now, actually, because that night we had together was the truest, most honest one of my life. And you should know there's no world in which I want to marry Calder Hawthorne. I've only ever wanted to marry you. *That's* why I'm here. To fight for you. For us."

He stares at me. The axe handle slides through his fingers, the head thumping into the ground.

My longing for him sharpens, becoming nearly unbearable. I want to leap from this saddle and straight into his arms. "I'm just sorry it took me so long to come. I should've done it right away, like you did for me. Better yet, I should never have left. I should've fought to stay. But I'm going to, now. No one's ever going to come between us again. Not my parents, or Brendan, or anyone."

He blinks. And stares. For so long that my scalp prickles. The only other time I've ever seen him hold so still was when my brother accused him of defiling me.

"Weston?"

He draws a long breath. "Birdie," he murmurs.

The nickname floods my insides with warmth.

"I think maybe you should come down from there now," he says. "It's not safe."

A glow brightens inside my chest. If he's worried about me, then he still cares. At least on some level. I grip the pommel and swing my leg over, then hop to the ground. "Is this better?"

"No." His jaw flexes. "That's not completely safe, either."

"Where, then?" I step closer to him. "Here?"

He shakes his head. Bright silver mingles with the gold in his eyes.

Another step. "Here?"

He presses his lips together. Another shake of his head.

I stray closer, until I'm standing squarely within his gravity, looking up into the same face I see when I close my eyes at night. "Here?"

"Not quite." He reaches for me. Pauses.

I hold my breath.

But then his arms settle around me, one at the small of my back, the other at the nape of my neck. He pulls me close, and I burrow against his sweat-slicked chest. I inhale until I can't anymore, then hold the tang of amber and salt in my lungs for as long as possible.

"Here," he says. "You're safe right here. For as long as you want to be."

I wrap my arms around his waist and squeeze, certain I've never heard such beautiful words before. "I don't ever want to be anywhere else."

We stand like that for long minutes. And, when I finally look up again, he isn't angry anymore.

Chapter Twenty-Six

T hat night, I marry Weston Wildes in Ravenfell, one town over, where no one knows our names.

The courthouse is unremarkable in every way, and the ceremony equally ordinary—just a few short words in front of the justice, followed by Weston and I signing our names in the registry. We have no bridal crown, no boutonniere, but we do have something infinitely better. The ability to hold hands the whole time.

It's perfect. An ordinary marriage for two ordinary people.

Afterward, Weston leads me to a charming inn with a gabled roof and a wooden sign hanging out front. We figure my father has probably reached the cabin by now, trying to put a stop to something that's already happened, and neither of us feels like dealing with it. So we'll stay here tonight. We can fight with him tomorrow.

Weston guides me through the door of the inn, his hand resting against the small of my waist. Inside, a rush of warmth and laughter envelops me. I take in the cozy common room, then move to unlace my cloak. And gasp.

Mud cakes my simple dress, the ugly brown standing out against the pale violet fabric. My gaze darts to Weston's black boots and pants, which are in a similar state.

"We're filthy," I say. "How'd we get so filthy?"

He studied me, quizzical. "By walking here? Why do you look like you've never stepped in a dirty puddle before?"

I blink at him. "Well. Probably because I haven't."

His brows lift, but a moment later, understanding smooths his features. "Ah. Right."

I inspect my dress again. I don't mind, really, it's just that I'm still adjusting to losing the litany of domestic conveniences I once took for granted. Some, I didn't even realize came down to luck. I never knew that clothes don't always stay perfectly folded when you dig for something at the bottom of the drawer, or that the oatmeal doesn't always run out just as your belly reaches its limit. Sometimes, you only get two spoonfuls, then have to hunt through the pantry for something more.

"Things are different for you, now," Weston says quietly.

I don't miss the hitch in his tone. I step in and brush my fingers against his jaw, coaxing his face down toward mine. "Not in any way that's important. I'd give my luck up all over again to marry you. A thousand times."

His mouth quirks, as if he doesn't quite believe me.

But I rise on tiptoes and capture his mouth with mine. He gathers me close, and I melt into him, letting the rest of the world fall away. When I finally pull back, he looks slightly more convinced.

"How is it for you now?" I say. "Not being a Null?"

He ponders. "Different. I can do all sorts of things I couldn't before. Build fires. Chop wood. The last time I tried to do *that*, when I was still Marked... A nail had grown into the tree, and a piece of metal flew off and got stuck in my eye. I had to come here to Ravenfell to get it taken out. Which was...not pleasant. But now..."

He trails off, his gaze going distant. "I can do things. I can *breathe*. It's peaceful. Easy. I don't know how else to describe it."

My chest lightens. Briefly, I remember the conversation I had with his alter-ego at the cabin, when he opened up about the challenges of being a Null.

"You should've let me kiss you ten years ago," I murmur.

His mouth tilts downward. "No, I should've been a gentleman and let you keep your triquetra."

I open my mouth to argue, but his tone has shifted into teasing territory.

"But lucky for me, I'm not a gentleman at all. I'm just a pugilist. And an accountant."

My eyes slide over him. In honor of our wedding, he's donned the black garb I've become so familiar with, sans mask. "And a highwayman. A very sexy highwayman. One I'd like to get kidnapped by again."

"Hmm." His eyes heat. "I think I'd like to take you upstairs, now."

I laugh. "I think I'd like that, too."

The innkeeper ushers us to our room. Once there, the man lingers, delivering a rambling speech about dinner hours and what to expect from this evening's entertainment.

I don't listen to any of it. I don't plan on leaving this room until morning.

When the door finally shuts, Weston makes for the bathroom. "I thought he'd never leave. Just give me a minute to get cleaned up, will you?"

I nod, my heart already spinning a hectic dance. Fortuna help me, the things I'm going to do to this man.

He shuts himself into the bathroom. I kick off my shoes and shuck my dirtied dress. Then I spread out on my back in the feather-down bed, waiting for my husband.

Goddess, my husband.

The word makes me so giddy that I swear a glow dances across the walls. I'm a lit ember, illuminating the room.

I close my eyes and smile.

A few moments later, a massive weight settles atop me. I open my eyes, only it's not Weston pinning me down. It's Jack. Black mask and everything.

"Where'd that come from?" I say. "Didn't you leave it behind the night you rescued me?"

"I had two. Any good highwayman always has two. Especially when he has terrible luck and is liable to lose one."

He almost-smiles, and I melt into the expanse of his gaze. Maybe his eyes remind me of honey, after all. Because he is sweet, in a way. Sweet and biting both, and I couldn't love the combination more. "Well," I say. "Whatever you're going to do to me, you should probably be quick, because my husband is around here somewhere. If he catches you, he'll probably break a bone or two."

"Mmm." He angles his face to nuzzle my neck. "I hear that's a habit of his."

"It is." A moan threatens to erupt, but I bite it back. "He's already broken eight bones in my honor."

He moves to the other side of my throat and licks, long and slow. I shiver.

"Strange," he says, gravel rattling in his voice. "I'd heard it was twelve."

I frown. He sucks on my neck, gently at first, then harder, until my toes curl. I force myself to concentrate. "It's eight, by my count."

"Then you're forgetting the guard. At Alverton's."

I blink and push on his chest until he leans away. "You broke four of his bones?"

He sighs, and I almost regret asking, because my neck feels very lonely, all of the sudden. "Just three," he says.

I do a quick mental tally. I may not be an accountant, but I can do basic arithmetic. "That's only eleven."

He holds my eyes for a beat. "Is it?"

My gaze thins. "Weston Jackson Wildes. What aren't you telling me?"

A soft laugh ripples out of him. "Fortuna, I'm going to regret telling you my whole name, aren't I?"

"Probably," I say. "Now who was the twelfth?"

He sighs. "Cameron Hale. Four years ago. He said you had great tits. And I didn't like that. So I hit him in the nose. It broke. The end."

I stare. I had no idea. None. "But...I *do* have great tits. So I don't know if that was really necessary."

He barks a startled laugh, then dives in for a kiss, which I grant him. By the time our mouths part again, we're both breathing fast, our chests heaving in synchrony.

"I'm the only one who gets to talk about your tits, Mrs. Wildes." Those golden eyes glint.

"All right," I say, breathless. "That's fair."

"And for the record," he adds, "I'm not going to be

hurrying anything tonight, vengeful husband or no. I promised we'd go slow. And you know what they say."

"What? Hope springs eternal?"

"No." He smirks. "Third time's the charm."

I search his face. At least the part of it I can see. Eventually, I'll make him take off the mask, but for now, I want him in that and nothing else.

"Even if there are no Charms here," he adds.

Before I can respond, he's kissing me again. I kiss him back. And I do indeed divest him of everything but the mask.

Then we learn each other, luxuriously, with teeth and lips and fingers and tongues. And I get my wish. I find out what he tastes like.

When he finally slides into me, I'm already half-drunk and sated. Our joining is unhurried, a gentle rock of our hips I never want to end. "I love you," he says, staring down. "I always have."

"I love *you*," I say. "I always will."

By then, it's just us—no mask, no clothes to shield us, no triquetras and no more doubts. Just me and my husband and the happiest night of my life.

When his lashes finally lower, fanning across his cheeks as his muscles cord, I lift my head and murmur in his ear.

"There may not be any Charms here, but I've been charmed twice in my life. Once when I was born, and again when I met you."

He clutches me close as he goes over the edge.

He doesn't let go.

Chapter Twenty-Seven

W hen we return to the cabin the next day, my father and Brendan are waiting, sitting astride their horses in the clearing. My father surveys Weston and me, his mouth tight.

I swing off my mare and give him a sorry-not-sorry smile. "You're too late. It's already done."

He nods, like he expected nothing less. "I don't suppose I can talk you into an annulment?"

I laugh. "Nope. It's too late for that, too."

He grimaces. That was probably crossing a line, but I don't regret it. Maybe I'll even make this a habit. Because it's better to cross lines once in a while than to live safely within someone else's borders.

Weston swings down and makes his way over to me, slinging an arm around my shoulders. The gesture is clearly a warning. A staking of claims. It's a declaration about how this is going to go, an expectation that my choice will be honored.

And I love him for it. A little more than I did this morning, a little deeper. He might still doubt himself, and I doubt myself, too, and we'll have to navigate our ways past that somehow, but when we're united like this, we add up into something greater than the sum of its parts. He believes in me and I believe in him and that makes us unbreakable.

"Any other questions?" my husband says.

My father sighs. Brendan winks at me, and I get the sense that they've already had a protracted conversation about this.

So I smile at my brother. It's the most genuine smile I've given him in years.

"No questions," my father finally says. "I don't know that I can argue with the law. Besides, Brendan had some valid points. I think maybe…we've been a little short-sighted with you, Bria. A little bit…"

"Selfish?" I supply.

He clears his throat. "Yes. But you should know your mother and I only wanted the best for you. Maybe we disagreed on what that would look like, but it doesn't mean we didn't care. So…I hope you're happy. I do."

"I am happy," I say, touched. "Deeply."

"Good. But you." My father fixes Weston with a glare. "You owe us a favor. An offering."

My husband straightens, his features settling into their habitual glower. "I don't owe you a thing. Not after what—"

"Not money." My father waves a hand. "Something else."

Weston tenses. "What else?"

Brendan's expression goes carefully blank. Quiet descends, filling the clearing.

"Go inside, Bria," my father says.

Weston's fingers tighten around my shoulders. "Whatever you have to say to me, you can say it in front of my wife."

My father matches Weston glower for glower, glare for glare. "Not this."

I pause, but there's something in the way he says it. A certainty that has me disentangling myself from Weston's grip. "It's fine," I say, and kiss his cheek. "Just hear him out. I'll be inside."

He nods, his jaw set. I leave them to talk.

I swing open the door to the cabin, step inside, and—

Stop. My hand flutters to my chest. I stare and stare and stare, tears misting my eyes. I can't believe what I'm seeing.

Many minutes later, when Weston finally joins me, I still haven't budged.

"When?" I say. My voice comes out rusty and tear-choked. I swallow down my emotions and try again. "When did you do this?"

He smiles shyly, then strides to the dividing wall. Which...isn't actually a wall anymore. An archway joins the two rooms, doubling the cabin's size. There's only one bed now, not two, and the bookcases sit side by side.

He runs a hand over the mortared stones of the archway. "I changed it before I came to see your dad. Do you like it?"

I blink the fog from my vision. "I love it. It's perfect."

"Good."

When the coil of emotion knotted around my airway uncurls, I wander close to him. "What did my dad and Brendan want? Outside?"

His features go blank, an eerie mirror of Brendan's expression from a few minutes ago.

"Weston?" Wariness edges my words.

"I'm going to go with them," he says carefully. "Right now. For just a little while. But I'll be back before dark."

I tense. "You're leaving me?"

He searches my face. "You'll be safe. I promise. Safer once I go than you were before."

I stand motionless, caught in his eyes. I know I can't rely on him every moment of every day. And while I'm still in recovery from my experience with the duke, I have to stand on my own two feet sometimes. Bold as brass.

"Okay," I whisper.

"But before I go," he says, "I want you to pick a number."

"A number?"

"Yes. Between...one and...two hundred and six, let's say."

I blink. "That's very specific."

A sharp smile slices across his mouth before vanishing again. It's unmistakably savage. "It is."

I hesitate. I almost consider asking for specifics, but I can tell he's not going to share them. "Twenty-three."

Something cold glitters in his eyes. "Twenty-three. Good choice."

He kisses me on the mouth, squeezes my hand, and retreats. At the door, he pauses. "By the way. We should go on a honeymoon. Spend a few weeks somewhere before I have to go crawling back to the cotton mill and see if they'll take me on again."

"A honeymoon? Where?"

His mouth tips. "I was hoping you'd have an idea. Why don't you think about it while I'm gone?"

I nod. And I do. And by the time he returns, many hours later, I have dinner ready, a fire going in the hearth, and the perfect destination in mind.

But Weston barely spares a glance for my efforts. There's a

crackling energy to him, one I've only seen a few times before, usually when he stepped out of the ring victorious.

"I made dinner," I say.

"Later." He comes at me like an aimed javelin, then picks me up and carries me to bed. And proceeds to love me with a ferocity that leaves me awestruck and breathless and deliciously sore.

Afterward, we eat, and he asks if I've come up with anything for the honeymoon.

I pause. I don't know how he'll take it, but there's only one way to find out. So I tell him.

He puts his fork down, thoughtful. "All right," he says. "I'm surprised, but all right."

Chapter Twenty-Eight

W e knock on Helena's door on a blustery morning in early November.

The door swings inward, and the moment she sees us, her brown eyes brighten. Her eyes drop to my collarbones, then to Weston's, and when she meets my gaze again, she presses a hand to her mouth. Tears quiver in her eyes.

"Hi," I say. "I hope this is okay. You did say we should come visit, and I—"

She yanks me into a hug, squeezing so tightly my words evaporate. "Of course it's okay. Fortuna, look at you. You look so beautiful. You both look so *beautiful*."

When she finally lets go, she turns to Weston. She approaches him slowly, every movement steeped in hesitation, but he doesn't resist. Helena ends up with her head buried against his massive shoulder, her eyes closed in gratitude. When she releases him, she and I are both crying outright.

"Fortuna's blessings," she says to Weston, between hiccups. "I never thought you'd let me do that."

SHAYLIN GANDHI

His face pulls into a glower. A mild one. "Well, last time you tried, you almost died for it. So."

She laughs, then pulls us into her charming cottage and insists on serving us tea.

While we sip, I tell her about everything that's happened since the last time we saw each other. Right down to Alverton and his terrifying room.

She sets down her teacup, her expression sober. "Well. It's a good thing he got what was coming to him, then."

"He...what?" I frown. "Got what was coming to him? What do you mean?"

Her golden brows pull into a line. "Didn't you hear? He took a fall from his horse. Two weeks ago. Broke twenty-three bones apparently, in the fall. He's very, very dead, Bria."

Shock stabs into me. I look to Weston, but he only gazes back, his expression mild. *Two weeks*. Right around the time we got married. Or maybe the day after.

My eyes narrow.

Later, as we lie in bed in Helena's guest room, I nestle my head in the crook of his shoulder and trace the swell of his pectoral. "That day, when you went with Brendan and my dad. Was that the same day the duke died?"

He aims a cool glance down at me. "Maybe. I wouldn't know. I hadn't heard about his accident."

"No?" I arc a brow. "So you wouldn't happen to know anything about his twenty-three broken bones?"

His expression doesn't flicker. "I wouldn't."

"Hmm."

He holds my eyes for a century, then aims a glance at where my fingers play with his chest, as if asking whether I plan to do anything more with them.

I absolutely do, but I have one more question, first. "Do you think," I say softly, "he broke those bones before he fell off his horse? Before he died? Or after?"

"Oh, before. That much, I'm absolutely sure of."

My hand stills. I just stare at him, my heart so full and wide that I have to go searching for my breath. Somewhere in the recesses of my mind, an awful little door to an awful little room clicks shut. "I love you," I say. "Goddess, I love you so much."

A small smile graces his mouth. Then he catches me by the wrists and flips me onto my back, pinning me to the bed in one move that has my head spinning and my pulse flying into a frenzy. My knees would probably give out, if I weren't already lying down.

"Anything else you'd like to ask me, Mrs. Wildes?"

"No," I manage. "Except…would you please kiss me, now?"

"Oh, what I'm going to do to you is much, much worse." He claims my mouth with his.

The kiss lasts and lasts, potent and needful and dazzling. I give it everything I have, and something about it feels like an awakening.

My life was once so small. I hid behind my Mark, hating it yet unable to look past it, and waited for someone to rescue me. Now someone has. Weston. But I also rescued myself, and now I'm fuller than I could have imagined. I'm not in the dark anymore. I'm no longer waiting. And, if I'm not quite bold as brass, I think I will be, someday.

Until then, I'm content to just be me. Bria Iris Wildes.

The luckiest girl in the world.

Bonus Content

For a bonus epilogue from Weston's point of view, and to see character art for *Once Charmed, Twice Cursed* (the carriage kiss!), visit **shaylingandhi.com/bonus** and join my mailing list.

Free swag packs with printed artwork, bookmarks, and signed book plates are available here as well (with purchase of *The Assassin's Song*, while supplies last).

If you enjoyed *Once Charmed, Twice Cursed*, check out Shaylin's gothic fantasy romance trilogy, beginning with *The Assassin's Song*:

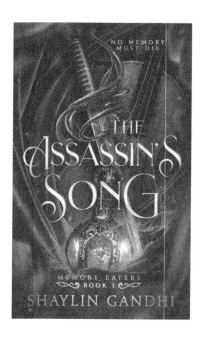

Cinder lives for revenge—she spends her days hunting the creatures who stole her brother's memories. But when a mysterious man promises to help restore her brother's soul, Cinder must venture into the dark world of the memory eaters. Now, to get her brother's memories back, she may have to join forces with one of the creatures she despises.

Good thing she has no chance of falling in love with him.

For More

For free books, bonus content, ARC opportunities, and subscriber-only sales, join my newsletter:

shaylingandhi.com/news

Also by Shaylin Gandhi

Contemporary Romance

When We Had Forever

Fantasy Romance

The Assassin's Song

Song of the Hundred-Year Summer

About the Author

SHAYLIN GANDHI is a traveler, scuba diver, and pianist. She lives in Denver, Colorado, with her husband, their identical twin daughters, and two rescue dogs. When not finagling words onto paper, Shaylin can be found hiking, biking, scheming up ways to add another stamp to her passport, or ingesting enough coffee to power a small city. Shaylin once spent forty-six days riding her bicycle from the Pacific Ocean to the Atlantic.

She can be found on Instagram (@authorshaylingandhi) or at shaylingandhi.com.

Made in the USA
Las Vegas, NV
13 September 2024